Nate Beck
was spread-eagled

His arms were pinned by knives piercing his biceps. His agony was intense.

"No!" Nanos shouted as he rushed to help his comrade.

An X commando stepped forward and bashed the butt of his rifle into Nanos's stomach. The Greek doubled over in his own agony. A fist smacked into his face. Then a second fist. Nanos crumpled and fell semiconscious to the floor.

Nate Beck's screams tore the night apart.

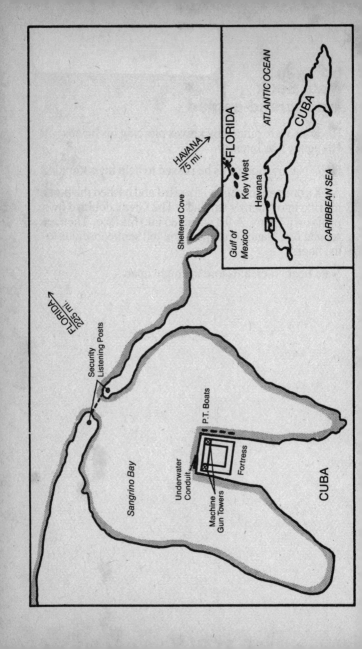

SOBs

EYE OF THE FIRE

JACK HILD

A GOLD EAGLE BOOK FROM

W☉RLDWIDE

TORONTO • NEW YORK • LONDON • PARIS
AMSTERDAM • STOCKHOLM • HAMBURG
ATHENS • MILAN • TOKYO • SYDNEY

First edition September 1985

ISBN 0-373-61608-2

Special thanks and acknowledgment to
Robin Hardy for his contributions to this work.

Printed in Canada

1

Colonel D. sat alone in his cell, waiting for the man from Havana.

It had been six months since he'd seen Buenos Aires, since he had strolled down the tree-lined Plaza del Major with his beloved Maria at his side. It had been six months since he'd been with any woman, for that matter.

Imprisonment was arduous, even without torture. He was fed and watered daily, and left to rot.

The thin, wiry colonel stroked his little mustache with one finger and abruptly stood up to pace for the umpteenth time that day. A white gull landed on the stone ledge outside his narrow window and peered curiously at him through the bars.

"Ah, my little friend. You know how lonely I am and have come to visit me, no?" The sea gull cocked his head and eyed the colonel.

"If you only knew who I really was—" the colonel fished for words "—then undoubtedly you would bring all your friends to meet me. I am a famous man, little bird. Yes, a very famous man." He could hear the sound of waves far below breaking against the base of the ancient prison.

He pounded his fist in sudden anger on the stone sill and threw himself against the wall in frustration. He was slipping into baby talk. Talking to the birds. That's what six months in prison had done to him.

The colonel swayed back and forth, rubbing his shoulders and the back of his head along the wall and staring off into space. A slide projector clicked inside his head, unrolling scenes of his past life. Clean, white-tiled, sterile rooms, racks of gleaming chrome instruments, classical string music playing from hidden speakers to calm him as he worked. His theaters of operation were his trademark, a sign of his professionalism. It was that rigid adherence to form and discipline that made him famous.

"Not famous," said the sea gull. "Notorious."

"You... stop it!" Colonel D. flew to the window and shrieked out at the bird. How dare it talk to him that way!

The disgruntled gull turned his tail feathers and flew off.

Colonel D. leaned against the wall again and sucked hard against the fist he held at his mouth. I must not allow myself to go crazy, he chided himself.

"Okay," he spoke out loud. "Not famous. Notorious. It makes little difference. My reputation precedes me. Men fear my name, little bird." He had begun to shout.

Fear the name of Colonel D. they did. The *D* stood for Diablo or Death, depending on whether one was an employer or a victim. Colonel D. was the master torturer of the Southern Hemisphere. He was an expert on techniques of clandestine kidnapping. His knowledge had grown extensive in the years he had spent traveling from country to country organizing death squads for those who paid him handsomely. There was scarcely a dictatorship in the Southern Hemisphere, military or otherwise, that had not benefited from his expertise.

Colonel D. stifled a sob and walked dejectedly to the narrow cot. He sat, his shoulders sagging with discouragement. If only, he thought, if only someone would come and rescue me. It seemed unlikely in the old stone fortress rising from a peninsula inside a small bay on the Cuban coast.

Influential people and powerful organizations owed him favors. He had stood by them. He had kept their secrets from his Cuban captors.

His brow furrowed, he twirled his mustache furiously between his twitching fingers. He pondered the fact that the Cubans seemed content merely to have him here. They had not tried to extract information. There had not been the slightest bit of torture. Perhaps they felt the torture master was immune to the methods that he had so frequently used.

There was just the man from Havana, who came once a week to sit and chat about the colonel's profession, his techniques, his bosses, his victims. Harmless subjects and inconsequential information. Sometimes the man from Havana said the oddest things, such as during the last visit when he had asked, "Have you ever imagined what your victims would do if they rose from the dead and pursued you?"

The colonel had laughed at this Hollywood notion of retribution.

But he disliked the sedatives. He rubbed his hand down the inside of his arm where the skin was punctured and hardened in places from the daily needles.

It was the one thing he objected to. The sedatives.

Sometimes during his conversations with the man from Havana he fell asleep. When he awakened, hours later, the man was gone.

Colonel D. sighed, swung his feet onto the bed and lay back, his hands behind his head. He studied the ceiling.

And waited for the man from Havana.

A FEW HUNDRED MILES AWAY from where Colonel D. languished in his Cuban prison, Tampa, Florida. sweltered in the humid June afternoon

In the smoky back room of a downtown pet shop, a man sat at a table, a second man paced and a third man leaned against the open back door. The air conditioner had broken down. The room was stifling. On desks, pushed up against the walls, a couple of typewriters sat among stacks of paper and light boards used for layouts. There was a telex machine in one corner, and a water cooler in another. The windows were barred. Pinned to the walls were copies of the front page of every published edition of a magazine called *Torch It! The Independent Voice for a White Christian America*.

The tall man who paced the room was Bob Braun, a retired U.S. Army major and presently editor in chief of the magazine he had founded. Bill Zetmer sat at the table. George Hampton stood by the back door carelessly holding an Uzi submachine gun.

The three men had met in the mercenary wars in southern Africa a few years earlier. They found they shared certain specific interests—killing Commies and killing scum. Often, but not always, the two were the same. All three were agreed on one thing: the Commies and the scum were destroying America, eating its heart out from within.

And the U.S. government, hog-tied by journalists and public opinion, was doing dick all about it.

That was where *Torch It!* came in.

Braun had a theory about making Third World intervention a private business. What the government couldn't do, mercenaries could. *Torch It!* acted as a clearing house, recruiting and advertising openings for professional soldiers in exotic locales the world over.

That took care of the Third World. Braun and his buddies had a more pressing and immediate problem—cleaning up America.

"I tell you," Bill Zetmer, a broad-shouldered, muscular man with sandy hair, said from the table, "Colonel D. will do the job for us."

Hampton laughed. He had a goofy laugh. Hampton was big but his weight wasn't fat. It was mass—big bones and stocky muscle. "Maybe I can teach him a few things, too!" He laughed again. Big George was a happy fellow.

"I doubt it," said Zetmer coldly. "Colonel D.'s the best. I know. I've seen him work."

Braun eyed Big George wearily. The guy was useful but annoyingly dumb. "It's time for it now, no question about it. A highly trained, mobile death squad right here in America will do a lot of good."

Hampton set his Uzi down, leaning it against the doorframe. He pulled his sweat-soaked shirt away from his massive frame. He was dripping.

"So you think it's going to work, Major?" he asked, strolling to the water cooler and grabbing a paper cup.

"Sure it'll work. As long as all the details are taken care of. A couple of days from now, Colonel D. will be safe here in America. That's why we are what we are."

Zetmer nodded. "X Command. The force of freedom."

"Even if that means freedom by force," said Braun.

Hampton laughed again and splashed ice water on his face.

"So what does..." Zetmer paused. The man he was about to name had no name. Braun knew who he was. To the others he was just an endless source of money for their operations. "What does our patron want with this guy Barrabas and his men?"

Braun shrugged. "The famous Soldiers of Barrabas. He wants them out of the way. So he's come up with the plan. We use them to do our dirty work. It will keep us out of danger and put them in danger. Lots of it."

"He wants them dead," Hampton stood with his hands on his hips, laughing.

"Suits me fine, too," said Braun. "I've got an old score to settle myself."

Zetmer stood up, bouncing a set of car keys in his hand. "It's my turn to relieve the other men on surveillance duty."

Braun nodded. "It's important to keep our eyes on Barrabas's men out at that beach house at all times, until we hear otherwise."

"Right." Zetmer started for the door to the alleyway. He stopped abruptly and turned to face Big George.

"Where's your rifle?"

Hampton looked at the door. "It's right there—" He broke off the sentence. It wasn't.

"Where?"

Hampton rushed to the door. "It's right..." He looked left and right. "I put it here, I just leaned it here a minute ago." He stuck his head into the alleyway. It was deserted.

The Uzi was nowhere to be found.

2

Nile Barrabas kicked open the door of the taxi, took his change from the driver and stepped onto the street. He had to walk the next few blocks because the driver wouldn't go any farther into what was considered a dangerous neighborhood in New York. The sky was gray; the air was as thick as a steam room's and stank of garbage. It was a lousy day. Everyone was after him.

His girlfriend wanted him in Europe for a little vacation, the Fixer was on his tail because he had a job he wanted done, and that morning, in his suite at the Plaza, he got a phone call from a woman in trouble.

Emilio Lopez's mother.

Barrabas walked quickly along the cracked, splintered sidewalks, through the smells and the sweaty summer heat. Blocks of empty buildings stood in rows like eyeless corpses, and a big fat man in rags pissed in a corner. The flood streamed over the curb, cascading past three winos sharing a bottle. Old sofas and mattresses spewed their stuffings and rusting appliances lay with their electrical guts ripped out. An old man rummaged through rotting garbage, surrounded by a pack of eight fat dogs who lay on the sidewalk like an infestation of hairy slugs. Their tongues hung out and they panted in the heat.

Devastation land.

A sign on a freshly painted building flashed a neon Jesus Saves. Maybe, thought Barrabas. City Hall obviously doesn't. He loved America but this part stank. When people had to live in a place like this, something was very wrong.

Usually it was a war.

And sometimes Barrabas had to curse the fact that he worked for the man with the gun.

He was the ammunition.

When the man said shoot, Barrabas and his soldiers went back to war. Back to the eye of the fire, that dead-hot center where the rest of the world ceased to exist. Place your bets and spin the wheel. Life or death. Him or you.

So far, countless times, Barrabas had won.

Once, Emilio Lopez had lost. Once was all it took.

Lopez, a seasoned soldier of fortune, had hired out with Barrabas. And, like the rest of Niles's men, Lopez was on the edge, desperate to get from fight to fight, battle to battle and war to war as fast as possible. To get to where you could forget the rules and blow the shit out of the bad guys.

The bad guys saw it the same way.

If you didn't kill them, they killed you. It sure made life simple. Barrabas knew it. So did Emilio.

The poor guy caught it from a grenade in the ammunition-filled hold of a cargo ship off Nicaragua.

All Barrabas brought home to the dead man's mother were heartfelt sympathies and half a million dollars. Lopez's wages for the job.

He walked past an old guy who looked like Santa Claus with a summer job. Selling sunglasses. Across the street, dark kids breakdanced to the blare of ghetto blasters the size of Japanese cars. He was getting into the heart of Loisaida, the Puerto Rican ghetto on the Lower East Side, and the street life was picking up. The upper floors of the five-story buildings were bricked up, but the first floors were used as an open-air clothing market. It was crowded and sweaty in the late-afternoon heat.

Her building was at the end of the street. It was like all the others. Five stories, brick, dirty. But all the windows had glass, and some even had curtains. The curtains hung out the open windows, limp in the humidity, and from inside came the sounds of a dozen different radio stations in grating counterpoint, an odd cacophony that would have brought them to their feet at Carnegie Hall. The metal fire escapes that crisscrossed the front of the building doubled as balconies, holding women with babies, little kids in diapers and shirtless tattooed men guzzling beers. Motionless, they all looked down and saw the tall, white-haired man looking up at them. They didn't smile. He was a stranger on their turf and they were letting him know it.

Barrabas pushed through the heavy front door into a small vestibule the size of a phone booth. The buzzers were on his right. He pressed Stella Lopez's. The door buzzed. He shoved it open and pushed into the long hallway. It was painted a glossy putrid green. He went for the stairs and quickly mounted to the fourth floor.

A tiny ancient woman wearing a heavy wool shawl opened the door. Her face was lined and cracked like ancient parchment. She shuffled back, looking at the big man, and tears streamed down her cheeks.

"Señor Barrabas, *ayúdanos, por favor*. Tony,

Tony.'' It was the grandmother. She didn't speak English.

Barrabas stepped inside the apartment and closed the door. It had changed little since the last time he had been here, the day he told Stella that Emilio was dead. It was clean and cluttered with oversized furniture, lamps with frilly red shades and big plaster statues of various saints and Caribbean icons. But the big plush sofa was new and so was the thirty-two-inch color television that blasted some game show.

Stella came into the living room. Her face was calm, but she clenched her hands and Barrabas could see the worry in her eyes.

''Nile.'' She walked to him and reached out her hand graciously to squeeze his. ''Please, sit.'' She gestured to the sofa. Stella Lopez was still a beautiful woman. Emilio had been a grown man when he died, and Stella had had her first baby when she was young. She was now in her forties, a beautiful slender woman with olive skin and luminous eyes. The man she'd lived with, Emilio's father, had disappeared somewhere along the way. Stella raised her kids alone with money she earned from the same job she'd had as a teenager. She had the sweetest voice on Manhattan Island. All the feeling from a hard life went into it. If she'd been black or white she'd have been a star. But she was only Puerto Rican, so she sang six nights a week at a corner bodega down the street.

Barrabas walked to the sofa. Granny was shuffling across the room, still crying. Stella took her by the arm.

''Excuse me a minute,'' she said. She led the old woman into a bedroom and returned.

''It's all my fault,'' she said, dropping into a big

stuffed chair. She was trying to sound collected, but
Barrabas could see tears glistening at the corners of her
eyes. She had three daughters, but Tony, her youngest,
was the only son she had left.

"I should have moved, Nile. I had the money. I could
have sent him to a good school, lived in a good place."
She stifled a sob.

"Now, hold on," Barrabas told her, his voice firm.
"What about the neighborhood? You told me you
wanted to stay here because this was where you grew up,
this was where your family and friends lived."

"Yeah—" she sniffled a little "—and I didn't want
him to get a bunch of fancy notions about who he was
like all those rich white kids who come down here looking for a place to live so they can be cool. I kept the
money a secret. Put it away for him and the girls when
they're older. I dunno, Nile. All I know is that he left
here sometime yesterday."

"Tell me about it from the start."

Stella shrugged. "He didn't come home. I found a
note in his bedroom. He said it was time to leave home
and be on his own. And..."

She played with the ring on her finger.

"And what?"

"The note said he was going to Florida to see Emilio's
buddies. That he was sorry and not to worry. Not to
worry!" Her voice rose with pain and frustration, and
she jabbed her hand into the air. "Not to worry! How
can he think his momma's not going to worry!" Stella
sighed. "Emilio left when he was seventeen, too. On the
very day. Tony was a little kid then. He barely knew his
brother. But Emilio used to come back with his money
and his pretty women. It was always a party for us when

Emilio came back. And Tony worshiped him. He always wanted to be just like him. When Emilio died, he just kept it all inside. So now he's gone off so he can be like Emilio, and he's probably got some crazy fantasy that he'll come back walking in a cloud of dollar bills with a pretty woman hanging on to his arm."

Stella shook her head. "But Tony's not like Emilio was. He's different, and he doesn't know it yet. He's not as tough, even though he tries to be." She looked directly at Barrabas, her warm brown eyes liquid with her plea. "Nile, he's going to get hurt."

"Does he know what Emilio did?"

Stella rose from the chair and walked a couple of steps away from him. "That he was a mercenary? I tried to keep it from him, but word gets around. Sure he knew." She turned back to face her dead son's commander. "Will you help, Nile?"

Barrabas stood and walked to her. He put his hands on her shoulders and squeezed gently to reassure her. "I'll help. Sure I will."

"Thank you." Stella crushed her face into Barrabas's chest. "You were the only person I could turn to. I knew I could depend on you. Emilio wouldn't have worked for you if you weren't a good man, Nile."

Barrabas moved back from her. "I'm not a good man, Stella. You can't be a good man when you're in my line of work. But I'll do it for you. And for Emilio."

Stella forced a smile and wiped her eyes again. "Coffee?"

"A fast one," Barrabas said. "Then I'll get on it."

AN HOUR LATER the sky was still light, but the shadows
had grown long enough to darken the facades of buildings. Stores were lit up by garish signs and vendors were
putting away their stuff and pulling down the iron
fronts on their shops. A tiny breeze drifted lazily
through the grimy hot streets. The brick and stone radi-
ated back the stored up heat of the day. The voices of all
the radios in all the windows were different now, a
chorus of loneliness in the growing dusk.

Gracefully and silently, like a deadly shark, a big
black limousine slid over the garbage in the gutters and
stopped smoothly at the curb as Barrabas came out of
the front door of Stella's building.

He did a double take and almost darted back inside.
But it was too late. Two fat fingers tapped on the window as it slid silently down.

Walker Jessup, also known as "The Fixer," stuck out
a chubby fist. The fist was shaking. The Fixer was
pissed off.

"Barrabas, I want you. And when I want you, I want
you fast, and I don't want to have to run all over New
York City looking for you. Understand me?" Jessup's
face grew redder and redder with each word. Barrabas
turned his back and walked up the street.

"Barrabas!" Jessup roared. The man kept going.
"Barrabas!" Jessup was going to burst a few blood ves-
sels if he got any angrier. Barrabas stopped. He didn't
want to kill the guy. He spread his hands in a gesture of
helplessness, but he didn't turn around.

"Jessup, I'm busy. I've got something to do. I don't
have time for Uncle Sam today."

The limousine silently came alongside Barrabas
again.

"Please come inside. Please talk. Please." The Fixer's voice was soft now. He was pleading. He was also almost dead from exhaustion. The man-mountain couldn't handle the heat. He lay back against the seat of the limo with his eyes closed, breathing heavily and mopping his forehead with a damp hankie. "Please, Nile. For old times' sake." He mumbled almost deliriously.

Barrabas took a two-mile hike around the enormous car and got in the other side. He slammed the door and heard the lock automatically click down. With an electric whir Jessup's window inched up, and the air conditioner started breathing down his neck like a polar bear on ice.

Jessup was breathing easier again. With his eyes still closed, he held the bridge of his nose with the tip of his index finger and his thumb, as if he had a terrible headache.

"You, Nile, are the cause of more grief, more trouble, more annoyance, and someday you will be the cause of my first heart attack."

Barrabas turned in silence and looked out the tinted glass window as the limousine pulled away from the curb and glided up the street.

"So what's with the big car today, Jessup? You always said limos were too noticeable."

"Not in this neighborhood, Nile. Look." Jessup tapped at his window again. They were going by a derelict apartment building. Half of it had been gutted by fire. The other half looked somehow inhabited. Another big limo was parked out front, and a white guy in a business suit was walking in through the big front doors. "Charity for some guys means coming downtown to buy their dope in the slums."

The driver's muffled voice came through the intercom. "Anyplace in particular, sir?"

"Just go where there are limousines."

That meant anywhere in New York City.

"Jessup, I don't know what you want me for, and I don't care this time."

"Nile, what do I always want you for? The House Committee in Washington has another problem, and they want you to bail them out. It's that simple."

"And I'm busy. I've got something else I have to take care of."

"Like chase after a runaway teenager because you feel responsible for his dead brother's run-in with a grenade?"

"Shut up, Jessup. I don't feel responsible. Emilio knew the risks when he signed up. But the family needs help, you know. Anyway, it's none of your business."

"You're right. It's not. But this is." He threw a photograph of a mustachioed Latin man into Barrabas's lap. "He was born in Argentina, and he's infamous. He's known as 'Colonel D.,' a nickname he got from the CIA. The *D* stands for Devil. Or Death. Until very recently he had a very profitable career giving lifestyle seminars in various Latin American countries. The life-style was terrorism and the seminars were about death squads and torture."

"So what?" Barrabas threw the photograph back into Jessup's lap and looked out the window. Now the limo was traveling quickly up the long, narrow, tenement-lined streets of Alphabet City. Avenue A. Avenue B.

"So now he's in a Cuban prison. The Nicaraguans

caught him six months ago training some Contras to do some very sick things to Nicaraguan peasants. They shipped him off to Cuba where he's been in prison ever since.''

"And you want me to get this guy out?"

"Wrong." Jessup looked directly at Barrabas. "We want you to kill him."

Barrabas threw up his hands. "Why do I bother?" The limousine was slowing in traffic, which clogged one of the narrow streets leading to Avenue B. Barrabas noticed that most of the other cars were limousines. Jessup was right. They were inconspicuous in the slums of New York. There was some sort of commotion on the sidewalk up ahead.

"For the money, Nile." Jessup had a way with words. A blunt way. "If he's not eliminated quickly he's going to blab. And he's got too much to blab about. On the other hand, the House Committee is just as happy that he's in prison and out of the way of American foreign policy, so they wouldn't authorize a rescue attempt. Only elimination."

"And they thought it might be up my alley. Jessup, how many times have I told you, I'm a soldier, not an assassin. Not an executioner. Get someone else to do your dirty work. Someone with bullets for brains. Besides, I'm busy, I already told you."

The limousine had come to a stop in the stalled traffic on Avenue B. Barrabas pounded his fist against the side of the door. "Open it, Jessup."

Jessup deliberated.

"Open it!" He slammed his fist against the door again. Hard. "Open or I break it."

"Open it," Jessup told the driver. The doors clicked.

Barrabas pulled the handle and stepped back into the heat.

A crowd milled on the sidewalk outside some big plate-glass windows on the bottom floor of an old tenement building. It was an art gallery. Everything beyond the windows was white and clean and stark and lit by spotlights. It was some kind of opening. About a hundred people, made up and dressed to the nines, stood around sipping white wine and yacking nonstop. On the sidelines, sitting on the stoops of their crummy tenements, blacks and Hispanics watched the wine-sipping white folks having a party on their block. Barrabas pushed through the crowd to get away.

The throng parted easily before the tall muscled man, but no one really saw him. He could have been carrying a chain saw for all they cared. They were too wrapped up in making the scene to notice.

"Barrabas!"

Jessup was running after him. Instead of slipping casually through the sidewalk crowd, Jessup's mountainous frame bulldozed through it, knocking people over. Wine from well-filled glasses spilled all over carefully assembled fashion accessories. People were giving him dirty looks. Barrabas turned and faced the Fixer again. The dozer braked. Everyone went back to their drinks.

"I want to puke." Barrabas's eyes narrowed.

"Why?" It was an honest question. He could see it in Jessup's eyes.

Barrabas curled his lips and motioned at the Letraset on the gallery's plate-glass window. "The name of the place."

The Fixer looked. The gallery was called "Civilian

Warfare." "I know what you mean," Jessup said. A waiter came out the door carrying a tray of champagne glasses. Jessup grabbed one with each hand as it sailed by. He slurped one down and offered the other to Barrabas. The big guy declined. Jessup slurped it back, too. He put the glasses on the hood of a limo idling beside the curb and patted his mouth with a hankie.

"Listen, Nile. You've been in this line of work for years. And before that you were a colonel in Vietnam. I know you've seen both sides of the U.S. government. There are good men and there are bad men. The bad men screw things up. The good men try to straighten them out. Look, I don't like the senator any more than you do. But he's the only connection we've got to the House Committee. I wouldn't come to you with this job if I didn't personally think it was legit."

"So?"

"So find Tony Lopez. You owe the mother the favor. For Emilio. Then let's talk. Just that. That's all I ask, Nile."

Barrabas thought a minute. He nodded. "Okay, Jessup. We'll talk again. In a few days."

Jessup broke into a wide smile. "And take this." He pulled out a red briefing case he had wedged between his elbow and his monumental torso. Barrabas eyed it warily. "Just have a look at it, that's all."

Barrabas took it. He felt like a fool. Completely sucked in. They called the man the Fixer because he knew his business. Then, something occurred to him.

"Jessup, how did you know where to find me this afternoon?"

Jessup's smile faded. He gulped and backed off toward the waiting limo.

"You tapped my phone at the Plaza, didn't you?"

Jessup grabbed the door handle and started to get in.

Barrabas went for him. A woman fell out of the crowd with a ferocious giggle and landed in his path. He placed his hand squarely on her back and pushed her back into the cocktail crowd. "That's illegal, Jessup," Barrabas yelled as the door closed.

Jessup smiled weakly behind glass and buzzed the window a few inches down. "Since when has that stopped either of us, Nile?"

Barrabas raised his arm to hurl the case.

Jessup buzzed the window up and the limo slipped silently away.

3

The iron gate at the end of the driveway wasn't locked. Tony Lopez pushed it open. He looked past the rows of shrubbery that led to the front door of the whitewashed Spanish-style house. It was the biggest house Tony had ever seen. And behind it, beyond the shade of the palms and orange trees, the sapphire-blue waves of the Gulf of Mexico washed up on the sandy shore.

Tony reached down, clicked off his stereo-cassette deck and took the earphones off so he could hear the long, even roar of the waves. A couple of times in New York City he and some pals had taken the F train to Coney Island where the ocean of people was bigger than the ocean of water. He'd seen nothing like this before. His face burst into a big happy smile. He knew it would be like this. This was exactly the kind of place Emilio used to talk about.

The ride in the Greyhound bus to Tampa had taken twenty-four hours. Then he'd walked miles to get to the place. He hadn't eaten since he spent his last dollar on an egg sandwich in Atlanta twelve hours earlier. But here, at the end of the line, he knew it had been worth it.

He looked quickly up and down the sunbathed street. On both sides the sidewalks were lined by high stone walls, wrought-iron fences or thick hedges that shielded the neighboring mansions from street view. Behind all this, life, albeit an air-conditioned one, went on. Except for a parked big blue car, the street was deserted.

Tony Lopez had arrived, but he was noticeably out of place in a neighborhood like this. His olive skin and dark hair, the blue jeans, T-shirt and sweatband, the little gold loop in one earlobe, made the five-feet-ten-inch youth look like what he was: a New York street kid from the Lower East Side. Some things were the same all over. In a neighborhood like this, some people would consider him a suspicious character. It was the way of the world. He hoisted his nylon rucksack over his shoulder and darted quickly inside the gates. Now he was out of view of anyone passing on the street. Halfway to the front door he stopped and surveyed the situation again.

It didn't look like anyone was home. It had that feeling about it. When he rang the bell on the big front doors, no one answered and the bell echoed inside the big rooms.

He tried the handle. The door wasn't locked. It swung slowly back, revealing a great expanse of polished floor. A glass wall on the far side of the house looked out on the beach and the white-crested waves rolling in. No one was there. But his brother's buddies wouldn't mind. Tony Lopez swaggered in without a second thought.

His white running shoes squeaked on the hardwood floor as he crossed the hallway. He'd never seen anything like it. It was definitely classy. Like the places people lived in on TV.

A stack of diving equipment was piled on the hallway floor: air tanks, wet suits, masks and fins. It all looked new.

He walked to the window and looked out across the gulf. Beyond the breakers on the thin line of blue at the horizon he saw a cruiser. He knew instantly that they were out there.

The scuba equipment was the other side of the equation. Tony Lopez put the earphones back over his head and turned his stereo back on. He decided to make himself at home.

CLAUDE HAYES WAS STANDING on the deck of the cruiser checking his chronometer to see how long Nanos and Beck had been down. The shrill beep sounded from the bridge. That meant someone had just violated the territory surrounding the house, setting off the electronic sensors. He and the two other mercs had rented the big oceanfront house for a month so they could do some private offshore diving training without being disturbed. Hayes taught them scuba and some underwater demolition techniques. It was his area of expertise.

The gate had been left open by mutual decision. Spetsnaz, the Russian military secret police, had already come after the mercs once on a mission of retribution. They were likely to do so again someday. Security of the human kind could be knocked out. Feigning carelessness and backing it up with security of the hidden electronic kind should be foolproof.

If not, they would have little time in which to be disappointed. They'd be dead.

It looked now as though this beautiful early-summer day was the one that Spetsnaz had chosen. Hayes walked to the bridge and flicked the transmission switch on the UTEL. A softer buzzing sound joined the shrill beep. The intruders had just entered the house.

NOT FAR AWAY, but at a depth of two atmospheres some sixty feet underwater, Nate Beck and Alex Nanos breathed slowly into the semiclosed circuit of the MKVI scuba gear. Nate heard Hayes's voice scratching through his earphones with a hollowness created by the aqueous depths.

"Marlin One to Marlin Two, can you read?"

"I read you, Marlin. Over." Beck spoke softly and clearly, his lips brushing against the microphone in the full face mask of his wet suit.

"We got a little problem. Unidentified intruders have entered the grounds and the house. Looks like we're going to see a little action today. Over."

"Coming up. Over and out."

Beck pressed the transmission button of the UTEL unit on his right hip and dropped the Bangalore torpedo he was holding in his left hand.

He picked up his harpoon-spring pistol from the ocean floor and kicked hard. His flippers propelled him slightly upward. He leveled himself out and began swimming quickly through the murky green darkness. He followed the thin, dull line of threaded Bangalores lying on the bottom. Somewhere out there, roughly six hundred feet away, was Alex Nanos.

Claude Hayes had trained them in the use of the semiclosed system of scuba equipment, which allowed them flexibility in the oxygen-nitrogen mixture they used. On this dive, the last in two weeks of intensive training, they were using a mixture that gave them a maximum diving time of three hours.

On each dive, Nanos and Beck had boned up on reconnaissance techniques. They worked in tandem doing some rough mapping of the ocean floor with high-beam lights and an underwater camera. On one of the last dives, Hayes had dropped down a box of Bangalore torpedoes for rapid-assembly exercises. Each five-foot-long, sixteen-pound metal rod contained Amatol and Chrystalline TNT. Ten of them linked together with standard firing devices threaded into the activators, made a chain a tenth of a mile long. Perfect for clearing underwater mines, sandbars, dead coral, or for causing a major amount of havoc in a marina full of pleasure craft.

Nanos and Beck had linked this set of Bangalores in only a few minutes. Still not fast enough, but they were getting better at it.

The dark underwater silhouette of Nanos's wet suit came into view. The Greek was slowly screwing the nose sleeve onto the end of the front torpedo. He was a good swimmer but still not used to the additional bulk of the equipment and the atmospheric pressure of the undersea environment. Both men felt as though they were moving through molasses at times. Nate got the hang of it faster than the ex-coast-guard navigator. Maybe it was because Nate had a kind of innate compatibility with machines—mainly of the electric kind with chips. But he seemed to be able to pick up on anything if it had an Off-On toggle switch and a couple of dials.

The scuba apparatus was a life-support system—the precursor of the space suit. When the diver went into the water, he entered a hostile world that wanted to kill anything without gills. Nate was fascinated by it.

Twenty feet from the Greek, Nate pulled his sheath knife from his belt and tapped twice on the length of torpedo below him. Twice meant stop.

Nanos heard the dull metallic knock come up the line

and looked in Beck's direction. He had his fist raised, then gave the thumbs-up sign. Surface.

Nanos left the nose sleeve half-threaded onto the end of the Bangalore. He grabbed his harpoon pistol and with a good kick shot up after Nate.

Both men switched from closed-circuit breathing, which recycled the air in a continuous circuit, to open breathing, so they could follow their escaping bubbles to the surface. The closed-circuit mode was obligatory for stealth and secrecy. Air bubbles breaking on the surface were a dead giveaway. And in the kind of circumstances these men were often in, a dead giveaway meant being dead.

Beck checked his watch. At a depth of sixty feet, they needed a minimum of a minute to ascend. He gave it another thirty seconds and paced himself. Nanos pulled up beside him. The Greek waved his harpoon pistol and shrugged and shook his head in sign language. No sharks today, either. Tampa Bay was supposed to be full of them, but they were staying away from these guys. Nanos was as disappointed as Beck was relieved. Nanos was hungry for a fight.

The two buddies swam slowly upward, six feet apart. Overhead the blue-silver mirror of the surface grew brighter. Fifty feet to the south it was broken by the dark hull of the 55-foot cruiser and the small speedboat tied up beside it. A school of sea bass sunning near the surface scooted off as bubbles heralded the approach of strange black monsters rising from the deep.

Exactly a minute and a half after they left the bottom, Nanos and Beck broke the surface of the ocean ten feet from the side of the cruiser.

Hayes was standing big, tall and black under the hot

Florida sun. Beck and Nanos tore the masks from their faces and pushed them up on their foreheads. Both men sucked back the fresh air, which tasted sweet after almost three hours on the tanked mixture.

"What's happening?" Nanos shouted at Beck as the two men treaded water.

Beck kicked again and stretched out an arm to front crawl to the side of the boat. "Intruders at the house."

Nanos didn't answer. He followed with a headup crawl to the boat.

A minute later the two men were on deck, unbuckling their webbed belts and stripping out of the wet suits. Hayes stood in the doorway to the cabin with two M-16s at his feet. He had a third one in his hands and was shoving a magazine into it.

"We can do this any one of a number of ways," the black man started to say.

"Or we can do it one way." Nanos gritted his teeth as he pulled the clammy rubber suit off his legs.

"Right," said Beck. "We can go in and blow the heads off whoever's gone inside the house."

"Sure, why not?"

Hayes nodded, then added sagely, "Though it'd be nice to ask a few questions first." He set down the M-16 and squatted to look at the two men as they pulled the wet suits off their legs and feet.

"We got the speedboat tied up here so we can get to the beach a quarter-mile down. They can't see it on the side facing away from them. We go in closer with the cruiser first, though, for a better look."

"And see who's spitting kisses," Nanos cracked, throwing his diving gear out of the way. "Have you checked it out with the binoculars?"

The black man shook his head. "If I look at them with binocs and they're looking at us, it'll alert them. Let's just nonchalantly go in closer and see what happens."

TONY LOPEZ was looking for something to eat. He wandered blithely into the kitchen of the great empty house and opened the door of the giant fridge. The gleaming white-and-chrome interior was empty save for a few dozen cans of beer. He took one, bounced it in his hand and ripped off the tab. It sprayed and foamed all over the counter and floor. He guzzled a mouthful. Then he burped and felt a little dizzy.

Tony Lopez knew all the moves. He knew how to walk like a man, talk like a man, drink like a man, and he figured he knew how to do a few other things like a man, too, because he'd seen it all on TV or at the movies. An automatic rifle? Just aim and fire. Grenade? Pull the pin and throw. It all seemed easy enough.

He sat for a while on the sofa, looking out over the beach and the rolling waves. The cruiser had turned and was moving toward shore. He felt anticipation hit him suddenly in the pit of his stomach.

Finally he was going to meet Emilio's buddies, the ones he'd talked so much about when he came back to the Lower East Side between jobs.

Several years ago Emilio went to prison, doing five to fifteen for using the coast-guard ship he commanded for marijuana pickups in international waters.

Stella just wrote him off. Emilio was the son that had turned out wrong. One day, Emilio turned up on their doorstep a free man.

He told Stella about his pardon. He didn't say how or

why, but Stella knew he was a professional soldier. She knew better than to ask. But word got around. Tony found out.

Emilio told Tony a lot about it. It was a secret between brothers. Those times when Emilio came back from missions with a guy called Nile Barrabas, he'd make Tony promise not to mention a word, then he'd tell him the stories. About how the soldiers of Barrabas rescued a black African prime minister from rebel captivity, how they nuked Iran and offed an international drug dealer in Sri Lanka. He told Tony about the battles, the brawls, the women and the good life between wars.

It all sounded grand, and sometime, Emilio promised, Tony could join up. But Emilio never came back.

Then Barrabas, the guy Emilio said he'd follow to hell and back, showed up. He was a tall man with short white hair and eyes that glinted like chips of ice. He told Stella the news. Emilio Lopez was dead. He died saving the lives of Alex Nanos and Claude Hayes. Hayes still kept in touch with Stella. That was how Tony had known where to find them.

Tony had waited a long time for this. And dreamed. Emilio had left home when he was seventeen. He'd gone from a street gang to court and got out of trouble by joining the coast guard. Tony waited until he was seventeen. That was his signal, his promise to himself. It was time for him to join the Soldiers of Barrabas, too.

He shook his head to clear the beer bubbles from his brain. Through the windows he could see the distant cruiser coming into shore. He set the beer down on a table in front of the great stone fireplace. He remembered seeing binoculars lying with all the equipment piled up in the hall. He got them, strode to the window and checked out the approaching boat.

The bridge and deck of the cruiser filled the sights of the powerful glasses. Tony felt a sharp thrill explode in his stomach when he focused on the men standing on the deck. It was them. The SOBs.

He recognized them from snapshots Emilio had showed him. There was Alex Nanos, with the dark curly hair and the physique by Muscletone, Inc. His nickname was "The Greek." He had been an expert navigator with the U.S. coast guard until he got the boot for not kowtowing to the top man. Emilio went straight to jail. Nanos and a big Indian guy named Billy Starfoot took up gainful employment as the most expensive gigolos on the East Coast.

Next to him stood another dark-haired, trim man. It wasn't the Indian, and he wasn't black. He didn't have red hair like Liam O'Toole, the Irish-American sergeant Emilio had talked about. So it must be Beck. Nate Beck, the Jewish guy from Queens, who used computers to rip off a million bucks. Emilio had neat friends.

Tony Lopez put down the binoculars. Suddenly he wasn't feeling good. His stomach felt like it had lead in it. Maybe it was the beer. His hands were sweaty. For the first time something occurred to him that he tried to put quickly out of his mind. What if they didn't want him here?

CLAUDE HAYES STOOD well back under the shadow of the covered bridge. He cruised the boat two hundred feet offshore and turned it parallel to the beach. Then he raised his binoculars and looked at the house. The grounds were empty and deserted. The house looked the same way. The sunlight glared against the windows and prevented him from seeing inside. He moved his glasses back and forth slowly until he saw something that gave the intruders away. Something glinted and sparkled briefly in the living room. It might be another pair of binoculars. It might be a gun.

He put down the glasses and walked to the edge of the bridge. "You guys ready?" he called down to the deck.

Nanos and Beck nodded. With their belts heavy with M-16 mags, they climbed into the flat-bottomed speedboat tied up beside the cruiser.

"Let's synchronize for fifteen minutes," Beck shouted up to Hayes. The three mercs checked their watches. Hayes took the wheel again and cruised the boat forward. The speedboat was hidden from view of the land. He took the cruiser to the far side of their property where it was partially concealed from the house by a string of palms on the shore.

"Take it away!" Hayes called to Nanos and Beck.

Nanos turned the key in the ignition and the 120 Mercury jumped to life. He eased the throttle open and geared forward. The boat sped away from the side of the cruiser and shot north along the coast. Simultaneously, Hayes opened the throttle full and spun the cruiser in a sharp circle.

The wake from the cruiser's twin inboard engines washed out the furrows left by the motorboat. With the cruiser turned, Hayes drove it south, paralleling the shore until he slowed to a halt a hundred feet from the house. He screwed a silencer onto his M-16. They lived in a nice neighborhood. He didn't want to bother the folks next door. He looked at his watch and waited.

Half a mile up the shore, private properties gave way

to open beach and the highway north of Tampa. Nanos cut the engine and brought the speedboat onto the beach, barely slowing it. Beck tilted the motor up as the fiberglass bottom coasted through the shallows and onto sand.

The two men jumped from the boat, pulling on bush jackets to conceal their M-16s. Beck ripped the cover off the engine and pulled the connectors off the spark plugs. He unscrewed one and put it in his pocket.

"So it'll be here when we get back."

"If we get back," added Nanos, under his breath.

The two mercs ran to the road and headed toward the house.

TONY WATCHED THE CRUISER come to a stop in front of the house a hundred feet offshore. The deck was clear now. He expected to see them throw out a rubber dinghy and make their way to shore. Instead, it looked as deserted as the house. Bored and restless, he put his stereo-cassette player earphones back on and paced slowly around the living room.

Ten minutes later, the boat out front still hadn't moved, and the batteries in his cassette player were going dead. Tony clicked it off and set it on the table beside the unfinished beer.

Something made him shiver suddenly. A noise. Barely audible, but he heard it. Someone had just opened the front door. He froze with fear. This wasn't turning out like it had in his imagination. He tried to remember how he had imagined it. Somehow he couldn't. He had assumed that his brother's friends would be here welcoming him. He had never filled in the details. He was scared. He looked around quickly for a place to hide.

Long curtains were bunched up against the wall at the edge of the window. He ducked behind them and held his breath.

He could see with one eye through a thin crack between the panels. Suddenly Alex Nanos spun around the corner from the hallway.

Tony's eyes went wide, and this time he felt weak with terror. Nanos was holding a rifle, and the rifle was big, cold and deadly. Lopez recognized it. It was an M-16.

"It's clear here," Nanos called out.

From the doorway on the other side of the room, Nate Beck appeared. He also held an M-16, and he looked like he was ready to shoot it. Finally something dawned on Tony Lopez with a sense of horror. They were looking for him.

His body stiff and his heart pounding inside his chest, he breathed slowly and tried not to make a sound. He didn't know what to do.

Then he saw something that doubled his fear. The can of beer and the cassette player sitting on the coffee table. Nate Beck saw them at the same time.

"What the hell is that?" He jerked his head indicating the find to Nanos.

The Greek walked slowly to the table with his back against the wall behind him. He kept the barrel of his M-16 fanning across the room in slow motion. "Hell if I know." He picked up the beer can. It was half full. Then the cassette player. He turned it over in his hand, then looked up, his dark eyes searching the room.

"Alex." Beck looked at the Greek steadily and with a slight movement of his eyes indicated the corner of the room on the far right where the curtains hung. At the foot of the draperies, a pair of white running shoes protruded. Nanos set the Walkman down, letting his M-16 fall slightly and veer to the right. It was set for a 3-round burst.

He pulled the trigger.

4

Washington D.C. sweltered in an unrelieved heat wave. The capital was built on a swamp and, as the temperature increased, the air got thicker and clammier and sweatier until a person could barely breathe.

The political atmosphere was much the same.

In his air-conditioned, oak-paneled office, the senator studied his secretary casually from across the vast expanse of his neatly arranged, leather-surfaced desk. She was taking dictation. The red nails moved quickly across the steno pad and glinted as if they'd been dipped in blood. The little steno pad did nothing to conceal her enormous breasts, curvaceously defined under the body-hugging jersey dress and revealing a hint of marvelous cleavage just below the collar. She looked at him, waiting for him to continue the memo. The senator sighed.

"Must you chew gum?" he asked her.

Her mouth stopped midchew, and for a moment she looked surprised. Then she regained her composure. She dropped the pencil, stuck her finger in her mouth and hauled out a big gobby mass. She plopped it into the large crystal ashtray in front of the politician. Unperturbed, she picked up the pencil, ready to begin anew.

The senator tensed and automatically pushed the Reverse button on his wheelchair. He whirred back from the thing in the ashtray as if it was radioactive.

"That's all for now, Miss Roseline," he said, turning his chair slightly and looking at his watch. "Fatso should be arriving any minute now. As soon as he gets here, show him in."

The senator was not one to mince words in private.

NOT FAR AWAY, huffing and puffing his way along Pennsylvania Avenue in the smothering blanket of humidity, Walker "The Fixer" Jessup, or as the senator would have it, "Fatso," was making his way to the politician's office.

Jessup had been called worse things in his time. And, besides, it was true. Too many years as a CIA operative and a half-dozen brushes with death had convinced Jessup that timely retirement and total indulgence were in order. Some men drown themselves in booze. Others in sex. The rest go for food. Jessup stood chins and shoulders above the rest.

Big as he was, there was more to him than met the eye. He was called the Fixer because he had a reputation for fixing things—Third World brushfires and peace treaties, the comings and goings of friendly or hostile governments, the neutralization of unaccommodating elements in inconvenient countries.

Various matters of minor significance.

All for a price.

Nile Barrabas was his main weapon. Barrabas got the job done, no question about it. Everything from nuking Iran to nixing a bloodthirsty Cambodian warlord who made Adolf Hitler look like the President's lady. On occasion, the problem was getting Barrabas to accept an assignment. He was reliable—but on his terms, and no one else's.

The senator's place in the scheme of things was, unfortunately, critical. The antagonism between the Fixer and the politician was mutual, but he was the link between Jessup and the House Committee that authorized covert actions and paid the bills.

The senator was old, rich, powerful and slippery. His instructions to Jessup were straightforward. And the hidden agenda was virtually invisible. Jessup cross-checked the assignments through his own network of friends, calling in favors to find out what was really going on. That was the problem with the Colonel D. assignment. The House Committee had definitely approved it, but there was no hidden agenda this time. It worried him. The slippery senator had something up his sleeve.

Jessup yanked at his necktie and loosened his collar. He patted the sweat off his forehead with a hankie. Then he went up the white marble steps and pushed through the glass doors. He stopped for a moment to offer a prayer of everlasting thanks to the gods for the invention of air conditioning. His suit was drenched.

A few minutes later, Jessup, still breathless and red from his walk, his suit stained and crumpled, walked into the senator's outer office. The new secretary was in the reception area. Jessup sized her up in one easy glance from top to bottom. He liked what he saw, but preferred to order his daily special in a restaurant. Meat on a plate didn't talk back.

He watched her light a cigarette and suck it between her full red lips as he came to a full stop in front of her desk. She flicked her eyes up coolly from the match just once and went back to lighting her cigarette, her lips drawing back hard on the thing until the head glowed red. She took it from her mouth between two red-tipped fingers and blew the smoke out over his head.

"Jessup, Walker," said Walker Jessup. He loved the way she looked so uninterested.

"The senator's expecting you," she said, returning the once-over. Jessup gulped. She was sizing him up.

"And he was right about you." She turned and opened the inner door. The senator was sitting at his desk. Jessup had to squeeze past the secretary's breasts to get through. She smiled at him.

"Miss Roseline, will you take these papers with you?" The senator held out a sheaf of papers. "Jessup, please come in and sit down."

Miss Roseline took a drag on her cigarette, crossed the room, plunged the butt into the great gob of salivated gum sitting in the ashtray and blew a cloud of smoke into the senator's horrified face. She took the papers from his outstretched hand, threw Jessup a sly wink and sauntered slowly from the room. Her timing was perfect. The door closed behind her like the end of a chapter.

"Walker, sit!" The senator's harsh command snapped him out of a reverie inspired by the beautiful behind. Jessup ambled to the chair and lowered his bulk into it. The senator's wizened face was dark today. The bushy gray eyebrows bunched together, throwing shadows over his eyes.

"What's his answer?" The senator got straight to the point. No time to waste on formalities. Or on politeness.

"No."

"What?"

"No. His answer is no."

The senator slammed his pencil on the desk, a token expression of his fury. "Jessup, I demand an explanation."

"One of his soldiers, Emilio Lopez, was killed in Central America when the SOBs went in to wipe out Jeremiah, the cult leader who tried to take over and ended up responsible for hundreds of people committing suicide."

"I am more than aware, Jessup." The senator's voice was scathing and he narrowed his eyes at the Texan. "I am forever aware."

The politician had paid a visit to the mad dictator to tip him off minutes before Barrabas had arrived. Jeremiah had died, but not before breaking the senator's back, which left him permanently in a wheelchair. Luckier than a thousand other bloated bodies that stank under the hot Honduran sun. Luckier than Emilio Lopez.

"Lopez's mother needed a favor from her oldest son's commander, since it seems her youngest son ran off and disappeared. Barrabas feels he has an obligation to help her out. He said he'd talk about it when he gets that done. But I'm warning you, Senator, Barrabas won't move at all if we put pressure on him. He's a stubborn man."

"Not stubborn, Jessup. Crazy!" the senator growled. "Then come back when he's ready. Until then there's no need to go over the details. But you might point out to Nile Barrabas that being a mercenary in America is technically illegal."

"Meaning what?"

"Meaning what I want it to mean, Jessup." The senator's threat was thinly veiled.

Jessup snickered and shook his head.

There were always going to be people in the world who thought they could deal with Barrabas. They learned the hard way. Jessup pushed himself up out of his chair and walked to the door. It was a short meeting.

"I'll let you know, Senator," Jessup drawled on his way out. He closed the door behind him and turned to Miss Roseline who was standing behind him with arms folded across her expansive chest. He squeezed past her. She turned to face him, smiling demurely.

Their eyes met and Jessup broke into a beatific smile of his own.

"How was the senator right? When I came in you sized me up and said the scumbag was right about me."

When she heard the word "scumbag" her smile widened. "He calls you 'Fatso.'"

Jessup's smile didn't disappear, it just faded a little. He nodded curtly and left without a backward glance.

Inside the inner office, the senator felt like a corked volcano stewing and straining to erupt. His rage was interrupted when a door in the wall behind him opened. A well-dressed man with slick hair walked casually in.

"You heard?" the politician asked with his hands out to indicate the helplessness of the situation.

The man dropped into the chair that Jessup had just vacated and swung his foot up over the arm. He studied his nails.

"No problem," he said smoothly. He looked up at the senator brightly. "We already know where the boy is. My people saw him go into the oceanfront estate a little while ago. He ran off to join his dead brother's buddies. Isn't that . . . heartwarming?''

"You have a plan?"

The visitor nodded. "We can turn it in our favor, and we'll be back to the original plan in no time. The irreplaceable SOBs, the troublesome Nile Barrabas included, will finally cease to be a problem. Permanently."

5

Tony felt the impact of the bullets through his shoes as the floor in front of his toes was chewed up by heavy metal. He ran like hell. Past Beck holding the beer can and Nanos holding the gun. He almost made it to the front door. Vice grips wrapped around his lower legs and sent him sprawling headfirst along the floor.

Alex Nanos and his flying tackle.

The opponents slid forward along the bare wood floor, Tony kicking madly to free himself as Nanos tried to get a better grip.

Next thing everyone knew, the three of them were standing and Beck was holding Tony's arms behind his back and yelling, "Hold it, hold it!"

He was talking to Nanos who was just about to plow the boy in the face.

Tony froze in complete fear. Beck gripped his arms tighter. In a second of sudden calm, Tony went on the verbal offensive.

"Hey man, what're you doing?" He drew his head back to put distance between himself and Nanos's threatened blow.

"Maybe you better tell us first what you're doing, punk." Beck spun him around and pushed him spreadeagled against the wall.

"I'm Lopez. Tony Lopez. Emilio's brother."

"What?" Beck stopped to look at him and waited for Tony to answer again. Tony looked from Beck to Nanos and back to Beck, where his chances of being believed were better. "I'm Tony Lopez, Emilio's brother."

Alex and Nate looked at each other. This was a twist that neither had expected.

"I came to visit," Tony said sheepishly.

Beck let go of his arm.

"Get in there and sit down!" Nanos pointed grimly to the living room. Tony swallowed and walked back in. The two mercs followed, picking up their M-16s on the way.

"Alex, you get Hayes. I'll baby-sit." Just as Nate spoke, the front door opened with a thud and the black American walked in.

He was barefoot, his dungarees were soaking wet and water dripped from around his coiled black hair like a halo. But the M-16 he carried was bone dry.

"I'm here," he announced. "Since you forgot about me, I surfed in." He strode on long legs into the living room. "What have we got here?" he demanded, looking the captive over. "You Tony Lopez?"

Tony was as surprised as Nanos and Beck.

"You were listening outside, weren't you? At the door?" Nanos accused in disbelief.

"No, man. He looks like Emilio. Can't you see?" Hayes turned to Tony. "Yeah, Emilio used to talk about his family all the time. What the hell are you doing here?"

"That's right," said Nanos, still steaming. "No brother or friend of Emilio's goes around breaking into people's houses."

"Hold it, Alex." Beck interrupted. "Let's face it.

Most of Emilio's friends did go around breaking into people's houses. Emilio was a great guy, but we all know what kind of friends he had. What do you want, Tony?"

"It's my birthday. I gave myself a trip to Florida." He looked at the three mercs. "To see you guys. Emilio used to talk about you all the time. I wanted to meet you."

The three mercs looked a little uncomfortable. Beck broke the silence. "Tony, this is a helluva welcome. You should have called first. To let us know. I'm Nate Beck." He stuck out his hand.

Tony looked at it, smiled, and shook it eagerly. Claude Hayes introduced himself the same way.

But Nanos was still ticked off. "Hey, we're busy here. We got things to do. We don't need some teenage kid hanging around."

"Alex, cool it. None of us is so busy we can't welcome Emilio's brother," said Hayes.

Alex thought a few moments, looking from Hayes to Beck. He nodded slowly as if he had been finally convinced. He put out his hand. "Yeah, okay. I'm sorry, kid."

Tony shook and looked Nanos square in the eyes. "I'm sorry, too. And I'm not a kid."

AN HOUR LATER, with the last glimmer of dusk dying quickly in the west, the mercs and Tony Lopez climbed into Nanos's car to drive off for something to eat.

"The Greek outdid himself on this one," Beck said gleefully as they climbed into the black T-bird convertible with white leather seats.

"And a 437 under the hood." Alex slapped the dash

and started the car. He winked at Tony. It had been grudging at first, but the two hotheads were becoming friends. "But I didn't buy it for the speed. I bought it for the ladies."

"Drive, Alex." Hayes reminded him. The Greek pulled out of the driveway and tore down the long avenue lined with palms and mercury arc lights. With the roof down, the Florida air rushed over their heads, warm and sweet.

For a moment Tony felt total bliss. Nanos talked loudly over the roar of the air. "Gotta girlfriend, Tony?" The Greek didn't wait for an answer. "I'll give you some tips. The car. Ladies like a guy with a classy car."

"You're listening to the expert, Tony," Beck said from the back seat.

"Damn right. The expert. I'll tell you something Tony, you listen to me—"

"And you, too, can be a ladies' man," interrupted Beck. "Alex you should have been a salesman."

"I was," Nanos said to the back seat. "I..." He stopped himself. He was about to say that when a guy worked as a gigolo, as Nanos had in the days before Barrabas had recruited him, he had to be a salesman. A fast-talking good-looker who could size a woman up, take her to lunch and leave her with the bill. And lunch could mean anything from a new suit to a new car.

He stopped himself from saying it. There were some things a seventeen-year-old kid was too young to hear.

"Anyway, Tony. A big car. And when they sit there in the cocktail lounge and order their banana daiquiris, flash the bartender a couple of fins and he'll make sure they're gin doubles. Buddy of ours used to call gin

'Ladies' panty remover.' Get it?'' Nanos winked at
Beck in the back seat. "Remember that, Nate? Biondi.
How he used to call gin 'Ladies' panty remover'?''

"I remember,'' said Beck, laughing at the Greek's en-
thusiasm. They'd been training for a long time.

They drove in silence for a few moments.

"Was he a friend of Emilio's?'' Tony asked.

"Sure was,'' Nate answered. Biondi was one of the
ones who hadn't come home again. Like Chen. Like
Wiley Boone. Like Chank. Like Emilio Lopez. No one
spoke for a while.

They reached downtown Tampa, such as it was. A
few gourmet food stores and several hundred discos.

"Perfect,'' said Nanos, sailing the T-bird smoothly
into the curb directly in front of the restaurant. "You'll
never guess what kind of food they serve here. It's really
unusual.''

The restaurant was classy. A porter took the keys and
drove the car away while another man who was dressed
like a cross between a five-star general and Michael
Jackson held the door open. Inside, the maître d' wore
white gloves and walked like he needed something in a
hurry. The mercs lived well between wars. It wasn't important to have a savings account in their line of work.
And spending it fast always meant getting back to work
before boredom set in. War was work, and for better or
worse, the supply was inexhaustible.

Hayes, Beck and Nanos took in all the plush surroundings without a second glance, except to check for
exit signs, escape routes, cover and clear shooting space.
It was reflex. Jerk reaction. So they could react to any
jerk who tried to take a shot at them while they were
eating.

"You'll never guess what kind of food they have here," Alex repeated after they had been seated. The waiter passed out menus like they were academy awards.

"Looks like kosher Chinese-Peruvian," said Tony, opening his.

Nanos looked suddenly disappointed. "How'd vou know?"

"I'm from New York."

"Why is it I'm surprised by these things that everyone else takes for granted?"

"Here, order for me." Hayes gave his menu to Nanos. "I gotta check in with Barrabas. It's eight o'clock." Hayes left for the telephones.

Tony watched him go. "The colonel?" he asked.

"That's right, Tony." Nanos looked absently up and down the menu. "One of us checks in daily. In case something comes up."

"You ever meet the colonel?" Beck asked.

Tony nodded. "At Stella's once. Stella's my mom."

"Does Stella know you're here?" Beck asked suddenly.

Tony swallowed. "What's good to eat here?" He studied his menu intently.

Nanos put his hand out and lowered the card from the teenager's face. "Tony?"

"Well," Tony started. "I left her a note. I said I'd be back...."

Claude Hayes returned to the table. He sat heavily and looked straight across at Tony.

"Yeah, the colonel was mighty interested in hearing you were down here," he said matter-of-factly. "He's flying down in the morning to see you." He looked around the table. "So what are we eating?"

After dinner Nanos drove them slowly up and down the main drag where the canopied entrances to the dance clubs and cocktail lounges came out to the curb, and the sidewalks were full of nightclubbers strolling in the hot evening. The Greek told Tony to check out how many women looked them over, to prove the wisdom of his taste in cars.

Then they went for a long drive down the coast highway. Nanos booted the T-bird so fast that the air whipped down on their heads and faces and the roar drowned out their voices. They ended up at a hotel-lounge on the coast, with a poolroom off the main lounge. The mercs wrote their names on the chalkboard for a game and passed the time eyeing the ladies and giving their informed opinion. Hayes rationed them strictly to one beer apiece. Tony drank Coke. Nanos kept nudging him to point out the lookers that cruised by and passed on more expert advice on how to be a ladies' man. Finally someone at the pool table called his name.

"You're up," said Hayes.

Nanos took the cue and shook hands with his opponent, the champion who'd been at the table most of the night. He set up the balls as the champ turned to his buddies.

"Watch me wipe this guy out," he boasted. His friends laughed.

Big joke. Nanos overheard.

"There's nothing I like better than death, baby!" Nanos roared across the room.

The champ took his turn first. He sank two striped balls. The Greek came up. He aimed for the solid colors.

When Nanos finished he'd taken care of all of them and sank the eight ball, as well. "Next!" he shouted.

Nanos stayed champion until eleven, when Hayes tapped his watch and ordered the mercs home to bed.

"We're training right now," Hayes explained to Tony. "And a soldier's no good even for training if he's out carousing all night long."

"Being a soldier is like every other job in the world," Beck added. "You have to keep learning if you want to... get ahead."

"You mean keep your head," said Tony.

"He's learning fast," said Nanos, returning from the pool table.

"From experience," Tony said in a low voice.

"What's eating you?" Beck asked.

"Nothing."

Later at the house, Claude Hayes stripped and cleared an M-16 while Tony watched.

"How do you know you put it back together the right way?" he asked.

"You know when you shoot."

"So, shouldn't you test it? You know, fire off a few rounds?"

"If you test it, it needs cleaning again. You just got to make sure you put it together the right way. Yeah, I know. You'd like to take a few shots with it. See what it feels like to fire an automatic rifle. Well, maybe tomorrow, Tony."

They were all in bed by midnight.

Tony lay back on the bed in the quiet house with the sheets half-off and listened to the distant, even roar of the waves washing up on the beach. He breathed deeply.

What was eating him was that he knew Barrabas and these other guys were going to put him on a plane back to New York as fast as they could buy a ticket.

And he'd just had the greatest day of his life.

And tomorrow it would be over.

Unless he could figure out a way to stay. A way to change their minds.

A couple of scenarios flashed in his mind. Persuasion? He could try. Make himself useful? How was he going to make himself useful to mercenaries who valued their freedom more than they did their lives? No, the best thing would be for something to happen. Something so he could prove to them that he had what it took. Like that blue car that was following them. None of the mercs seemed to notice it. But the car that had been parked on the street when he had arrived that afternoon had also been parked outside the restaurant at dinner and at the hotel when they left. He was pretty sure it was the same one.

If he had just a single chance to prove himself—and one of those M-16s—Tony was sure he could make the grade.

Visions of heroism danced in his head as he drifted off to sleep.

6

Not far from where Tony Lopez lay dreaming, another teenager with similar ambitions wandered down a street in suburban Tampa. Unlike Tony Lopez, this one did have a gun—the Uzi that Big George had so carelessly left lying around.

And tonight he was going to use it.

The air had cooled a little so the dark green nylon jacket that hid the Uzi didn't look obvious. Nor did the fatigue pants tucked into his jackboots and the grunt cap he pulled down to shade his eyes. He dressed that way all the time.

Jimmy Jollimore, nickname "The Kid," was a tall, gangly nineteen-year-old. At high school and in the neighborhood his keen interest in guns and all things military was well-known. One day at school a guy named Wally Garvis said, "He thinks he's a big man. Let's call him 'The Kid.'"

"Sure," he told them all. "Call me 'The Kid.' 'Cause I ain't kidding around."

Wally Garvis was a big-mouthed Commie and he was going to get it.

The Kid couldn't believe his luck. It was like fate intervening on the side of justice. He went down that alleyway that afternoon because he wanted to check out the office of *Torch It!* The guys who wrote for it had

some good ideas about how to deal with scum. He
wanted to meet them.

As he approached the back office through the alleyway, the alluring metal sheen of a rifle, standing in a
doorway all by itself, caught his eye. It was everything
he'd ever wanted. Someone had heard his prayers and
put it there just for him.

He took it.

And when he got home, he discovered the mag was
full. Now he was going to make a dream come true.
He was going to go over and blow Wally Garvis's head
off.

Always smile for the man with the gun. I'm the man
with the gun, now. He laughed to himself.

Finally he came to Wally's house.

The curtains were pulled across the long picture window of the ranch-style dwelling, and the house was lit
from soft lights within. The Kid looked around to en-
sure no one was watching. Then he darted quickly up
the driveway and stood in the shadows under the carport. He pulled out the gun and set it on semiauto.
When the time came, he didn't want to waste bullets. He
only had one mag.

He circled silently around the house, peering in
darkened windows. One was lit by the flickering blue
light of a television. He approached stealthily. Flattening his back against the side of the house, he turned his
head and peered inside. Wally Garvis sat on a couch in
the rec room watching TV.

The Kid ducked under the window to continue his
circuit. When he got back to the carport he hid the
gun under the nylon jacket again and rang the door-
bell.

The muffled sound of voices and footsteps came from within. It opened. Wally Garvis stood there.

"Kid!" Wally was surprised. Kid was hardly a friend. "What are you doing here?"

"Hi, Wally. I thought I'd drop by to say hello."

"Uh...oh." Wally looked uncertain as to what to do. "Wanna come in for a Coke?"

Kid smiled. "Sure."

Wally stepped back and held the door open as the Kid stepped into the house.

"What's the matter with your arm?" Wally asked, noticing the stiffness where the rifle was concealed.

"Nothing," Kid said. "Uh, I fell off my bike today. It's a little sore."

"Who is it, Wally?" A woman's voice called from the living room.

"Just a friend from high school, mom." Wally turned to Jimmy. "Come on down to the rec room. I was watching TV."

The teenagers went down a couple of steps and walked down a corridor to the TV room.

"I'm kind of surprised you came to see me, Kid. You're sort of a loner at school," Wally said on the way.

Kid didn't answer. When they entered the rec room, he closed the door behind them.

"Oh, you can leave it open," Wally started to say.

Kid pulled out the Uzi. "No, I can't, Wally."

Wally looked at the gun and looked at the Kid.

"Yeah, it's for real." Kid looked Wally straight in the eyes and pointed the rifle at him. "It's for killing Commies, Wally. Commies like you."

Wally put his hands out in front of him and started to back away. "Kid, look..."

Then the door opened.

Wally's mother was there.

"Would either of you boys like some..." She stopped talking when she saw the rifle. "What's going on here...?"

Kid turned and pulled the trigger.

Three bullets instantaneously smacked her body into the hallway. She jerked on the floor then lay with her head at an odd angle as a great lake of blood spread silently and quickly underneath her.

Kid turned back to Wally who had frozen in terror. Their eyes met. Jimmy's were deadly.

"No!" Wally screamed and turned to run. Three soft pops from the Uzi knocked into the teenager's side. He slammed against the wall with one hand to steady himself. He wasn't dead yet, but it was there. In his eyes.

He turned to the Kid. Kid fired again. Bullets pierced Wally's chest, leaving blood splats on the wall behind him. Wally slumped to the floor, shuddered and was still. His eyes, wide and empty, contemplated the ceiling and the flickering light of the television. A guy was talking about his deodorant.

Kid looked from one body to the other. He was momentarily stunned that he had actually done it. Stupor melted into elation. He broke into a big smile.

Then he heard footsteps coming up the basement stairs at the other end of the house. A male voice called out.

"Hey, Wally, you got the TV on too loud." It was Wally's brother, a couple of years older. And he was going to see the body in the hallway.

Kid rushed to the door. The pool of blood made the carpet squishy, like grass after a heavy rain.

He heard Wally's brother swear.

"Oh, shit! What the..."

He'd seen the body.

Kid pivoted out the door, falling over the corpse and aiming straight down the corridor. He pulled the trigger on full auto.

Bullets slammed out, chinging into plaster and wood and smacking into the bone and flesh of the third victim. His face caved in and he smashed back against the wall. He fell down slowly. The body groaned on the way. Then he was still.

The house was still. Except for the guy selling deodorant on TV.

Kid looked at the carnage. His fatigues and boots were smeared with blood. He didn't seem to know how it got there. My first battle, he thought. My baptism of blood. Too bad the mother and brother got in the way. But it was war. People died.

A few minutes later he was off, running through the back alleys of the suburban neighborhood and feeling the cool winds of night against his face. His feet hardly seemed to hit the ground as he ran, and he sucked back great lungfuls of air. He felt like he could run through the night forever, almost as if suddenly his feet would leave the ground and he would fly. He had never felt so high in his life. It was the greatest high of all. High on the kill.

IN THE SMOKY BACK ROOM of the Tampa store, the men of X Command were gathered. Two of them were angry. The third was contrite.

"George, how could you be so stupid?" said Bill, who paced angrily by the table. "How many times did I warn you to take better care of the gun?"

"Half a minute! I just left it there half a minute while I had a glass of water."

"I don't care how goddamn long you left it there. The point is the gun is gone. And who the hell took it? How do we know it isn't one of those prying newspaper reporters. Then they check the registration, find out it's illegal and bust our asses." The short, muscular man slammed his fist into the palm of his other hand.

Major Braun sat at the table, brooding. He wore a shoulder holster that carried a vintage Luger engraved with swastikas. It was the pride of his collection. "Some nosy reporter comes around here, he's got to deal with me. And I'll give him what-for to deal with. Like a lawsuit that'll clam them all up for a decade."

He turned to face the other man at the table. "George, you're an asshole and this proves it. The organization is going to have to discuss disciplinary action. But right now there's no point in getting riled up about a whole bunch of imaginary consequences. We've got an assignment from the top, with class-A priority. So let's move on it."

"The boy," said Bill. "Tony Lopez." He pulled a chair out from the table and turned it to sit backward, folding his arms over the back as he faced the other two men. "If the kid ran off, then they'll probably send him home to momma soon. If we're going to catch him, we got to act fast."

Tom nodded. "Barrabas is arriving tomorrow morning at Tampa International Airport. That's when we'll do it. We keep the house under steady surveillance.

When they go to the airport with the kid, we'll nab him there.''

"What if they don't take the kid to the airport?" George asked.

"If they don't, we'll go in the house and take him there. Either way, it's tomorrow morning." Bill said impatiently.

"Shhh." Braun hushed them suddenly. He cocked his head and listened intently. Silently he moved across the room to the back door. He put one hand on the well-oiled bolt and quietly drew it back. He placed his fore-arm and open hand flat on the door and with a sharp, hard shove, pushed it open.

The thick door struck pay dirt as it flew outward. A body went tumbling back into the night. The light from inside poured over a man sprawled on his rear end in the gravel. Then Braun's six-foot shadow blocked the light. He looked down on the eavesdropper with his Luger drawn.

He cocked the pistol, slowly and deliberately for maximum effect. "Now get up with your hands in the air, or I'll blow your goddamn head off."

The figure started to rise. The hands were way up. "H-h-hi." It was a nervous voice that belonged to someone very young. Then Braun saw the Uzi lying on the ground.

"Decided to bring it back, did you?"

"I'm on your side," Kid said eagerly.

Bill and George moved up behind Braun. Their leader circled the fatigue-clad teenager. "Don't move," he commanded. His voice was deadly. He reached down and picked up the Uzi.

"Get inside."

Kid did as he was told. Braun followed with a quick backward glance. He slammed the door securely shut and bolted it.

The three men took a good look at their captive in the light.

"What the hell...?" Bill started to say. All the men saw the blood-drenched fatigues.

Braun grabbed Kid by the collar and pulled him roughly across the room. He pushed him into a chair.

George pressed the cold steel barrel of a Magnum steadily into Kid's right temple and cocked it.

It all happened so fast, Kid didn't notice the urine spreading through the seat of his pants and flowing onto the floor.

"Steady, George, the kid just pissed himself." Bill was laughing at the terrified teenager.

"Start talking," Braun ordered, "before we send your brains flying in lumps across this table. For a start, where'd this gun come from?"

The words poured out of him. "I took it." His eyes flicked fearfully back and forth among his captors. "This afternoon I saw it there. I took it. I'm sorry."

Their eyes weren't growing any friendlier and his head was aching where the cold circle of Magnum steel pressed.

"I'm on your side. I just killed some Commies with it. Like you said in your magazine. It's war."

"Jesus Christ," Braun muttered. "George, relax."

The big man lowered the Magnum and stood back.

"Put your hands down, and tell us what you did."

Kid told them.

The three men listened in silence. When he was finished, Bill and George looked at Braun, waiting for him to talk first. Braun said nothing.

"What're we going to do now?" Bill asked, looking accusingly at George. "This is what you've got us into. Major Braun, what we gonna do?"

"We gotta kill the kid," George said quickly, standing up from the table and pointing. "It's the only way. We can't turn him in." He held up his Magnum and aimed it at the Kid's face.

"George!"

George looked up at Braun. The leader had his Luger leveled on a line that ended between George's eyes. "Put the gun down."

George lowered the gun. "We can't let him go," he sputtered insistently.

"He's right!" Bill joined in.

"Shut up! Both of you!" Braun shouted. "Sit down!" Braun pulled another chair over and sat, as well. He kept the Luger out and aimed vaguely in the Kid's direction.

"What's your name?"

"Kid. That's what everyone calls me."

"Naw, your real name."

"Jimmy. Jimmy Jollimore."

Braun nodded. "Okay, we'll call you the Kid. Kid, you wanna kill Commies?"

Kid nodded eagerly.

Braun looked at the other two men. "I think we can use him for the time being. On that urgent assignment we have tomorrow morning." He turned and looked Kid over again. "We can reevaluate his usefulness afterward."

The other two men seemed surprised.

"I got you, Major Braun." Bill nodded understandingly. "You're brilliant. Yeah, Kid. You wanna work for us, we might let you live."

"Right, Kid," George joined in. "Either that or..." He leveled his Magnum across the table. "Pow!" With his thumb he silently sent the hammer home.

7

Claude Hayes eased Nanos's big black T-bird into a Standing Only space at the front of a long line of waiting cars outside the main terminal of Tampa International Airport. Tony looked glum sitting in the front seat beside him. The warm fresh air of the Florida morning wafted across the open top of the car. An airport cop immediately trotted over to point out the No Parking sign.

"No sweat, Officer," said Hayes. "We're just waiting for my mother from Toronto."

The cop looked suspicious but wandered off to check meters.

"You're sending me back, aren't you?" Tony said accusingly.

Claude put the car in reverse and looked over his shoulder to back up and straighten out. "Tony, I don't know. Let's wait and see what the colonel has to say." He braked, disengaged the gears and turned off the ignition. "Look, you're gonna have to go back sooner or later. You just don't run off to be a mercenary when you're seventeen. If you want to hang out with some of us, that's great. There's nothing we'd like better. But right now we're training. It's not a good time."

"Or, as Alex said, 'We don't have time for you, kid.'"

Hayes gave him a friendly slug on the shoulder. "Forget what the Greek said. Come on. The colonel's plane touched down a minute ago. Let's go find him."

"Sure. Leave the car here?"

"Yup. Tickets are on Alex today."

The New York street kid slung his bag over his shoulder and followed the big black man to the front doors.

They sank into the coolness of the conditioned air inside the vast terminal building. A disembodied voice from on high was announcing the arrival of the New York flight.

"Over there," Hayes pointed to the escalators to the upper level.

"I'll meet you up there. I gotta take a leak."

Hayes looked at the teenager, for a moment doubtful.

"Hey, you think I'm going to run off or something?" Tony laughed. "Where?"

Hayes laughed, too. "Sorry. Meet you upstairs."

Tony crossed the terminal toward the service area marked by the Ladies and Gents stick figures. On the way he saw something that made him green with envy. A guy about his own age was all decked out in camouflage gear, the legs of his pants tucked inside the tall laced-up boots and the rim of his jungle hat pulled forward to shadow his face. Tony couldn't help staring as he passed by. The kid stared back with a friendly smile.

A few minutes later, Tony was looking in the mirror over the sinks and adjusting his sweatband. The guy in the camouflaged fatigues walked in, carrying a thick, heavy duffel bag.

Once again, their eyes caught.

"How're you doing?" the young man said to Tony.

"I'm okay." Tony bashed the heel of his palm against the electric dryer and put his wet hands under the stream of hot air, while the other kid went to the urinal to do his business. Tony flashed him a shy glance. The kid at the urinal twisted his head around to look over his shoulder.

"You waiting for someone?"

"Yeah. Sort of."

"So'm I."

Tony concentrated on drying his hands. The stupid hot-air machines never worked. Press button, hold hands under hot air, rub gently, wipe hands on pants. The air went off. Tony bashed the button again.

"Yeah, I just came in from Chicago," the other teenager said. "Came down to do a job." He finished at the urinal, did himself up and came to the sinks. He watched Tony in the mirror as he washed his hands. "Yeah, I got a real good job this time around."

Tony couldn't resist the bait. "What kind of job?"

"What does it look like? I'm a private soldier. Used to call us 'mercenaries' until the government and the journalists made it a dirty word. So we call ourselves 'private soldiers' now."

Tony looked at him, not quite ready to swallow it.

"Don't believe me?" the youth said, wiping his hands on his pants. "Look, I'll show you."

He reached down and unzipped his duffel bag, pulling some clothing away from the top.

"Wow!" Tony gasped, wide-eyed. The dull gleam of deadly metal was a submachine gun.

"It's an Uzi. My name's Jimmy. But everyone calls

me the Kid.'' He leaned over and quickly zipped up the duffel bag.

''My friends showed me how to strip one of those and put it back together, last night,'' Tony said as coolly as possible.

''Oh, yeah? You in the business, too?''

Tony nodded. ''Uh, yeah. With my friends. We have a house out on Ocean Drive we're using for undersea divers' training.''

Kid nodded.

''How'd you get this job?'' Tony asked as casually as possible.

''Connections. Just like you. You must know that.''

Tony nodded as if he understood everything. May as well go for broke, he thought. ''Yeah, actually I'm looking for work right now.''

''Yeah?'' Kid hoisted the duffel bag over his shoulder without looking at Tony. He didn't sound interested.

''Yeah. We just finished a job. In Cambodia. You know how it is. I get kind of restless between wars.'' It was a line he'd heard his brother Emilio use on more than one occasion.

Kid looked at Tony. ''Hey, I think my friends are looking for one more man. They might go for you. Come and meet them.''

Tony couldn't believe his luck, but he feigned a casual disinterest of his own.

''Come on,'' said Kid, heading for the washroom door.

NILE BARRABAS WALKED smoothly along the incline of the long tube that led from the airplane to the arrival lounge. He ignored the stares that his height and muscled physique drew. He was used to that kind of attention. He got it from women because they liked what they saw, and from men because they didn't like their wives looking and because a man like Barrabas reminded them of their own failures. When Barrabas walked through a crowd it was with the gait of a fighter. His blue eyes were accentuated by his closely cropped white hair. The face, still young, was marred here and there by scars as if the chisel that had carved it had occasionally slipped. One scar ran high along his left cheek and disappeared into the hairline just past his temple. It was a reminder of the bullet he took at Lap Long in the crazy Asian war. It had pierced his helmet, then his skin and finally his skull, coming to rest about a millimeter short of death or bona fide vegetable status at the local veterans' hospital. As it was, Barrabas cashed in one of his lives, took the scar and the permanent whitening of his hair for a receipt and went on to fight another day. Many other days, it turned out.

Through the immense plate-glass walls of the arrival lounge, Barrabas could see out across the wide, flat runways to the tall, spindly palms of Florida's west coast, the blue sky with its little puffs of June clouds and the friendly yellow sun that the locals worshiped like a god.

He looked around for some sign of his men just in time to see Claude Hayes rise smoothly into view on the escalator.

"Good to see you, Claude." Barrabas gave him a friendly slap on the back. The two men walked slowly away from the crowds of arriving passengers and their noisy greeters. "How's it going?"

"We're just about finished, Colonel. Nate and Alex

have picked up the basics of scuba and underwater demolition pretty fast. Especially Nate. I got a few more things to show them and then they can practice on their own wherever they go next.''

''And where's that?''

Hayes laughed. ''The Greek is itching for a few weeks of hell raising and he says he's going to terrorize the Caribbean from Key West to Aruba in his search for the perfect woman.''

Barrabas chuckled. ''And Tony?''

''He's downstairs, Colonel. Waiting for us. And he's not too happy about going back to New York City.''

The two men reached the down escalator and stepped on.

''Can't say I blame him, Claude.''

''He's a good kid, Colonel. I was thinking, I got nothing to do in a few days when I finish with Nanos and Beck. I could show him around here. Do some fishing. Try to talk him out of some of these ideas he's got.''

''You mean about being a mercenary.''

''Uh-huh. These kids see it on TV and read those magazines and they think all they need is a machine gun to go out there and lead a genuine exciting life. Jee-sus, Colonel. I'd like to take them on a tour of Cas'n Hatton the day after Spetsnaz came to visit.''

Barrabas winced at the memory. The SOBs had holed up at Lee's Spanish villa while the Russian military intelligence miniarmy came after them. The miniarmy was minimized. There were only two left when the SOBs finished with them. But Lee's estate became a slaughter-ground, the villa was dynamited into smithereens and the Eskimo pilot he'd hired got blown into two perfect pieces, bottom and top.

As the escalator continued its descent, the two mercenaries had a panoramic view of the downstairs terminal floor. "That's Tony over there." Claude pointed.

They could see the boy talking to a couple of men. A third person was younger and decked out in enough soldier gear to win the door prize at a costume party. They were approaching the end of their descent. Lopez stood with his back to them about fifty feet away, close to the front doors of the terminal.

"Who the hell's he talking to?" Hayes wondered out loud. Barrabas was thinking the same thing when one of the men in the little group looked around. His eyes locked with the colonel's.

"I know that guy! Let's go!" Barrabas leaped down the steps of the escalator three at a time, deking right and left to cut through the other passengers. Hayes was right behind him.

Braun, the man Barrabas recognized, casually spoke a few words to Tony Lopez. The little group started walking outside without a backward glance. Then Braun reached under his jacket and pulled out a gun.

In the vast terminal building with its hubbub of traffic and noise the shots were muffled into slow, echoing snaps. Barrabas and Hayes leapfrogged over the side of the escalator with six steps still to go and did a shallow dive for the floor behind a stack of luggage a tour group had piled in the middle of the terminal. Barrabas heard the bullets smack into the soft leather cases.

There was a temporary lull in the noise level of the terminal as people looked around to see what was happening.

Someone noticed the bullets shredding through their suitcases. They screamed. Screaming is contagious. So is mayhem. With the word "terrorist" riveted in every brain, businessmen and tourists, women and children began running helter-skelter across the polished floors looking for any kind of cover they could find. In the wide open space of an airport terminal, there wasn't much. Airplaneloads of tourists from the north pushed and shoved one another just to get behind the spindly trunks of a few emaciated potted palms.

Barrabas got across the floor and shot out the big front door with Hayes behind him.

The two men panted behind the great portiere as security guards ran the wrong way into the terminal.

Up ahead, a black Oldsmobile screeched away from the curb and tore off down the outramp.

"This way, Colonel!" Hayes shouted, running for the T-bird. The two men leaped over the open sides, with Hayes jamming the key in the ignition and bringing the engine to life with one long fluid motion.

"Check out the panels," he yelled, driving the steering wheel hard to the left and booting the gas pedal. The T-bird roared with pleasure as the engine guzzled back gas and they shot forward onto the road. A hard left curve complete with an ear-wrenching screech and the smell of burning rubber swung Barrabas against the passenger door. He reached down below the padded handle where his fingertips felt the thin line in the fabric cover and touched the cold steel barrel of a Smith & Wesson K-38. Nanos always did like the big guns.

The T-bird screeched again as it slid onto a ramp at the airport entrance. It surged forward onto the freeway. The black Oldsmobile was a half-mile ahead, but they were gaining.

Barrabas propped himself by sitting up high on the

back of the front seat with his body forward. Both
hands steadied the gun as he aimed it over the top of the
windshield. He narrowed his eyes against the impact of
the wind, which flattened the skin of his face.

He pulled the trigger.

And missed. Hayes had to change lanes to avoid rear
ending a little old lady who might have been from Pasa-
dena.

It was almost impossible to get a steady aim on a target as small as a rear tire when the T-bird was doing 140
up the freeway. He could shoot in the general direction
of the Olds, but someone could get killed that way. Like
Tony Lopez.

"Parallel them," he shouted at Hayes over the noise
of the wind.

Hayes was braking and swerving amid the loud honking protests and screeching tires of other cars. The Olds
was in a clear stretch ahead. Hayes pulled the T-bird
over the front line of traffic and floored it. The car shot
ahead. Hayes pulled it across two lanes to the inside left
then veered across four lanes to arc around a long curve.
He reached the top of the curve late and put his wheels
close to the outside right lane. It slowed him slightly going into the turn, but he was able to exit with greater
speed.

He pushed the T-bird through a smaller string of traffic, resulting in a chorus of honks and raised fists once
again. Finally he brought the car out in the front line
once more, with the black Olds only fifty feet ahead.

Neither Barrabas nor Hayes could make out Tony
through the glass of the back windshield. What they did
make out was an arm holding an Uzi coming out the
back passenger window and spraying the road in front

of them. Both men squirmed down behind the protection of the dash, keeping their heads up just enough to see the roofline of the other car.

Another autostream socked back at them, pounding into the car's metal frame. Hayes didn't slacken speed. Barrabas suddenly lurched up with the K-38 in his right hand and aimed out the side of the car. He sent two bullets on a trip to the Olds, low and against the trunk. He still wasn't going to risk hurting Tony.

The gap between the two cars closed to ten feet with both vehicles in the inside left lane of the freeway on a stretch free of other traffic.

A dozen cars hogged the lanes about a quarter mile ahead, unaware of what was coming fast on their tails.

The T-bird bridged the gap, when suddenly the driver of the Olds spun the wheel and the car jumped to the right, crossing four lanes of freeway in a near straight line and speeding off down an exit ramp.

It was too late for Hayes to make the turnoff.

The black man let out a war whoop. "Hold on, Colonel!" He braked suddenly, slowing the T-bird down to half the speed. Then he turned the steering wheel a half turn to the left, simultaneously grabbing the emergency brake and pulling on it hard.

With a shrill screech, the ass end of the T-bird fishtailed, throwing Barrabas back against the seat and sideways against the driver. The hubcaps flew off in all directions and clattered across the highway. Barrabas pushed himself up as the car turned ninety degrees toward the oncoming traffic. Hayes released the brake and straightened the wheel.

Now they were heading in the other direction.

The wrong way on a one-way freeway strip.

With a phalanx of cars with horns shrieking bearing down on them, Hayes floored it.

Some braked, others veered quickly out of the center lanes cutting off drivers behind them. Hayes roared the T-bird through the opening in the front line until he was on the other side of the turnoff.

Then he did it again.

He turned the steering wheel to the left and hit the emergency brake. For the second time, the T-bird fish-tailed out and Hayes brought it around in a 180-degree turn. He accelerated down the ramp just as a second line of honking traffic zoomed past.

Hayes and Barrabas didn't notice.

They were down the ramp. It took them onto a secondary road that wound its way through a long strip of take-out food joints and hardware stores. The black Oldsmobile was nowhere in sight.

8

The black Oldsmobile came to a stop in an empty parking lot behind a drive-in bank. Major Braun and Bill Zetmer in the front seats exchanged relieved glances.

"Close," said Braun. "Very close."

"Okay, Tony, you can come up now," George Hampton said in the back seat. He grabbed the teenager roughly and hauled him up from the floor to sit between him and Kid.

"Sorry, Tony," Braun said, looking around. "We wanted you down in case we took a line of bullets across the back window. At least until we get you your own gun."

Bill turned on the car radio and disco music hummed from the dashboard.

"Who were those guys?" Tony asked, glancing over his shoulder and out the back window. He wasn't entirely convinced their pursuers were gone.

"We are staking out a possible terrorist action at the airport," Braun explained. "But they saw us first. It means they were tipped off."

"Terrorists!" Tony was awed by his brush with the real world of action.

"Yeah. A Cuban organization," said Kid. "So I told you no shit and I meant it."

The disco gave way to the twelve o'clock news. The

lead item was about the bodies of a mother and two sons found brutally murdered in their suburban home. Braun, Zetmer and Big George exchanged nervous glances.

The Kid listened. Bill leaned over and clicked the radio off.

"Hey, my buddies do this kind of work, too. Maybe you guys know them. Alex Nanos, Claude Hayes and Nate Beck. And the colonel's name is Barrabas."

"Yeah, sure, Tony. The SOBs. We work with them sometimes. A great bunch of guys," said Major Braun.

This time Tony swallowed it. Hook, line and sinker.

NANOS FREAKED when he saw the car.

Hayes rolled the T-bird up in front of the big house. The Greek took one look at the convertible and his eyes went wide with shock.

"Holy hell! What did you guys do?"

"Stopped off at a demolition derby, Alex," said Hayes, crawling out of the driver's seat.

The hubcaps were conspicuously absent, the front fender and side sported a line of bullet holes and the tires had fringes from the moonshiners' turn.

Nanos circled the car, too shocked to mutter anything more than the same swear word over and over. Barrabas and Hayes pushed past him and headed for the house.

"Phone's in here," Hayes said, leading the colonel into the luxurious living room. Barrabas cast his eyes quickly around the room and took in the view of the beach and the cruiser anchored offshore.

A moment later the Tampa–New York line crackled with long-distance static.

"Jessup, I want a favor."

"No way, Barrabas. I got no chits due. Not unless I

get a commitment that you're going to work on this little job we talked about.''

"I'll think about it, Jessup."

"Thinking will not get the job done."

"Screw off."

"Is that what you want?"

"Awright, Jessup. Just listen. A seventeen-year-old kid who thinks he's going to be a soldier superstar is in deep trouble. I came down here to meet him this morning and while I was getting off the plane he got swiped. I missed a date with some bullets from an Uzi. Claude and I managed to deduct about ten years from the lives of a few hundred freeway drivers in the chase afterward. They got away. I need some information, Jessup. Fast.''

There was a long silence on the other end of the line.

"What in hell's going on, Nile?"

"That's what I want you to tell me."

"What do you have to go on?"

"A name. I recognized one of them at the airport before the shooting started."

"Who?"

"His name is Braun. Bob Braun. He used to be a major in the U.S. Army, I think. I ran into him as a mercenary. It's a small world out there in the war business, and you get to know all the major players after a while. I came across him in Angola. Apparently he was a recruiter. One day in the field, my men and I came across the bodies of women and children machine-gunned and thrown into body piles six feet high. Everyone said it was Braun and his friends who did it. But no one could prove it."

"I've heard the name, Nile. Weren't there stories

about him shooting his own men when they balked at his orders?''

"Yeah, that was another story. But you know how it is. Sometimes it's hard to tell truth from what's real in the middle of a war. Can you get me some info on him fast?''

"Nile, this is going to cost me."

"Put it on my bill."

"I don't mean money. I mean favors. The kind that don't have a dollar value."

"So, all right, Jessup. I'll do you one sometime."

"Okay, Nile. Soon as this is all over with."

"Soon as it's over with."

Barrabas hung up.

An hour later, the phone rang. Barrabas picked it up, made a few noises and put it down. He turned to Hayes. "It was Jessup. He's on his way down."

Then Barrabas checked his wallet for a number and dialed New Jersey.

A thousand miles or so away, in a suburban living room just off the freeway into Jersey City, the phone rang. Liam O'Toole had barely finished tonguing the pretty blonde's right earlobe and was working his way down her neck and around to her left.

"Leave it!" she sighed wistfully, arching her back as O'Toole drove his tongue and lips against the tender skin of her soft throat. The telephone rang again.

She relaxed her body while strengthening her embrace around the Irish-American's muscular shoulders, pulling him down onto the couch.

His hand slid from her full breast down the flat of her stomach to her navel, where he spread his fingers apart and clenched her tightening abdomen.

The phone rang again.

"Don't answer," she pleaded, breathing the words out heavily as she stretched her head back to bare her neck.

He was almost up to the left earlobe when he realized it might be for him. The colonel had this number now. Liam O'Toole had fallen in love with the horniest woman he'd ever met. They weren't living together, but they never left the house.

It rang again. Persistent.

O'Toole's hand reached out over the arm of the couch and grabbed the receiver halfway through its last jangle. He raised his head slightly and growled hello into the mouthpiece. Then he twisted it out of his way and dive-bombed the blond woman's neck like a vampire.

He didn't get far this time.

The voice in his ear was terse, the voice of authority. It was the colonel. And the colonel was giving orders.

O'Toole sat up quickly. The blonde breathed heavily and sank back, her eyes gazing at her man and waiting for him to return.

But her man didn't have time for her anymore. His attention was riveted on whomever was on the phone.

"Right, Colonel. I'll be down on the next flight out of here. Probably in three or four hours."

Liam O'Toole reached over the woman to hang up the phone.

"Gotta go, Susy." He looked sorry. "I told you this would probably happen again."

She smiled a little, giving in to what she realized she could do nothing about. "Guess I'll have to start getting used to it, won't I? I hope so. I mean, I hope you'll come back and stay with me."

O'Toole's face lit up. "Will I? Susy, I don't ever want to leave. Not now, not ever. But. . ."

"But a man's got to do what a man's got to do. Right?" Her eyes were teasing.

O'Toole looked embarrassed. "I guess," he said. "At least I used to need the kind of work I do. Now, with you, I don't know. Maybe you're all I need."

"I doubt it, Liam," she said, raising her arm and running her index finger lightly across his lips. "Besides. . ." Her arm dropped and she looked at him.

"Besides what?"

"It's a small price to pay for a guy like you."

Back in Florida, Barrabas hung up the phone and paced across the living room to the window looking over the Florida beach. Hayes waited for him to speak.

The front door slammed shut and Nanos walked angrily into the room. Nate Beck was right behind.

"Hey, awright you guys, I want an explanation for the car. The car is a wreck. What the hell—"

"Shut the hell up, Nanos!" Barrabas shouted, turning angrily from the window. "Just get the goddamn car fixed. Right now we got a more serious problem."

Nanos shut up. He looked from Hayes to the colonel and back to Hayes again. "What's going on?" he asked darkly.

"Tony Lopez was either kidnapped or ran off with some men at the airport." Hayes explained. "We tried to stop them but they had guns."

Nanos bowed his head and looked at the floor, speechless. "Sorry," he said. "I just. . . I just blow off like that and don't think."

"Forget it, Alex," Barrabas said, any trace of anger gone from his voice.

"So what's happening?" Beck asked, pulling a chair out from the wall and sitting.

"I recognized one of the men who took Lopez. From the mercenary wars in southern Africa." Barrabas said. "I got the Fixer working on it. And O'Toole's on his way."

"What about the others?" Beck asked.

Barrabas shook his head. "There's no point in calling up Bishop and Hatton until we know what's going on ourselves."

"Yeah, up at his little love nest in Canada," Nanos commented.

"Alex, you are one hell of a sore loser," said Hayes. "Lee was into Bishop long before you even thought about making it with her."

Barrabas kept his silence on this one. Geoff Bishop was his ace pilot and Lee Hatton was the woman warrior and medical doctor on the team. The two of them met on a mission in Central America, and their affair was a secret—a public one. Alex Nanos had got it in his head that Bishop had moved in on his territory. It was a dumb idea. Lee Hatton was out of his league. But it strained the fighting relationship between Nanos and Bishop. Barrabas wanted to avoid a crisis there as long as possible. They were both good soldiers and he needed them.

"What about Billy Two?" Beck asked, breaking the lull.

Barrabas shook his head. "Billy's not right anymore," he said sadly.

There was another lull, this time with each of the men going into mental territory that he tried to stay out of as much as possible. Sometimes on a mission a buddy got killed. What happened to Billy Two was worse. Spetsnaz

had drugged him and tortured him until he lost a piece
of his brain. Loony-tune time. The six-feet-five-inch-
tall, full-blooded Osage Indian wasn't the guy they'd
once known, the fighter who tagged along on their
whoring sprees between the wars. Billy Two was stark-
raving mad.

"We'd never find him anyway," said Nanos, walking
to the sofa and throwing himself heavily onto the over-
stuffed cushions. "Last I heard, he was out in New
Mexico or Arizona somewhere taking care of family
business, he said. More likely he was there to crawl into
the desert and howl at the moon."

"Colonel, what do you think is going on?" Beck
asked. "Why Tony Lopez?"

The big man paced across the room to stand by the
window. "I don't know. Maybe it's all just an accident," he said. "We'll know when the Fixer gets here."

He looked out at the steady roll of the waves from the
Gulf of Mexico. A pelican glided calmly over the water.
Suddenly it jackknifed and plunged headfirst into the
waves. A moment later it rose from the water with a fish
flapping its life away, wedged firmly in the bird's beak.
Pelicans always kept their eyes open, even when they
dived into water. Eventually the saltwater blinded them.
Then they starved to death.

Barrabas had the distinct feeling he'd walked into
something with his eyes closed. He didn't know what
was going on, but his memories of Major Braun in
southern Africa weren't good ones. He would long
carry the afterimage of corpses of women and children
and old people heaped up like firewood outside their
burning village and human ears flapping from the belts
of the soldiers Braun had commanded.

Braun had always managed to cover his ass, too. Barrabas remembered the one conversation they had had, word for word. He had faced Braun in a crop field, ankle-deep in blood, and spoke hoarsely through the dark, acrid smoke of the burning village.

"Goody-goodys like you bug me, Barrabas." Braun leered at him. "Bleeding hearts are assholes."

"I'm going to nail you, Braun. Maybe not now. Maybe not soon. But I'm gonna nail you."

"Not if I get you first. And I got lots of guys who'll pull the trigger happily." Braun turned and disappeared into the bitter, swirling smoke.

Years later and half a world away the memory washed in and out while Barrabas gazed at the ceaseless roll of the gulf waters.

Tony Lopez was definitely causing him a great deal of trouble.

But something else was going on. Lopez was a very small part of a grand plan. What the plan was and whose it was, was a mystery. He had a gut hunch about it, though. Barrabas knew they were after him.

MANY MILES DUE WEST of where Barrabas stood looking out over the Gulf of Mexico, a man sat cross-legged and alone on a hillside in Arizona's desert.

He was naked save for a beaded headband, which held his long black hair away from his forehead, and he was protected from the ground by an intricately woven mat of Navaho design. In front of him, tiny flames burned in a small brass urn. He took some dried leaves from the mat beside him, crushed them in his big hands, then sprinkled them into the urn. The little fire smoked as the dried leaves caught. The man leaned forward and inhaled deeply. Then he sat back and relaxed, his arms limp at his sides, his hands resting on the ground, palms up.

For one week Billy Two had sat here, naked and alone in the desert. Once a day an Indian woman from a nearby village brought him water. Other than that, he had not eaten or drunk anything. Nor had he shifted to shield himself from the hot sun or the chill of the desert night.

He fasted and meditated, and his mind wandered and contemplated. He was waiting for a vision, the vision of Hawk Spirit, the warrior god of his people. Hawk Spirit had come to him twice before. Once in a psychiatric institute in Moscow when Spetsnaz doctors had injected him with sulfazine to burn his body up from the inside out. The second time was in a courtyard in Barcelona where Billy Two had managed to burn his Spetsnaz guards from the outside in.

Since then, Hawk Spirit had not returned. For a week Billy Two had prayed and fasted and contemplated, but nothing had spoken to him but the great silence of the desert...and the bear growling in his empty stomach. It had been growling there for days now. The previous night he had begun to sweat as if he was burning hot. Now, under the hot sun, he felt chilled, and shivered.

He leaned forward once again and took another lungful of the dwindling smoke. He closed his eyes. The vapor from the herbs made him light-headed. He felt as if he was floating six inches above the desert sand. Streamers and sparklers flashed across his closed eyes like a psychedelic color chart. But still no Hawkeye.

Then he felt something.

A presence.

Someone was approaching.

Billy Two brought his hands in slowly until they rested against the side of his body. His fingers stretched out until they touched the weapons hidden under his thighs. In the left hand the handle of a knife. In the right, the handle of a Browning AutoMag.

Billy Two breathed deeply. Perhaps it was Hawk Spirit. He opened his eyes.

He was wrong.

But not in left field.

It was Emilio Lopez.

Emilio was tanned and healthy, his white teeth gleaming under the thin Latin mustache. He was smiling the typical Lopez happy-go-lucky smile. He looked like he was glad to see his old friend Billy Two again.

"You're trying too hard, Billy!" Lopez said after they gazed at each other for a minute.

"Are you Hawk Spirit?" Billy asked, thinking perhaps this was merely one of the many different forms assumed by the warrior god.

"No way," said Lopez, shaking his head sadly. "That old buzzard, he kind of does what he wants. No use sitting out here in the desert making yourself sick and waiting for him to do a house call. It doesn't work that way."

"But the ways of my people—"

"Sure, sure. Go out into the desert and smoke this stuff and you'll have visions. Uh-uh. The ways of your people are gone. Forgotten. It's all new now, Billy Two. You have to start all over again."

"But you are here."

Lopez nodded. He looked unhappy.

"It's time, Billy Two."

"Time for what?"

"Time to see your friends. They need you."

"Need me? For what?"

"I need you, Billy Two. There are some things—" the apparition's voice faltered "—I can't do anymore. You have to do them for me."

"Tell me what, Emilio."

Lopez shook his head. "Go, Billy. Quickly." At that moment a great cloud of thick white smoke burst from the little brass urn as if something had been thrown in. The white smoke quickly rose into the air where it was rent by the desert wind and scattered into the growing dusk. The apparition was gone.

Billy Two stood up. The sun had just fallen behind the barren hills in the west, leaving a carmine tide to flood the sky. The desert sand turned pink and the cacti and shrubs that stretched out across the flatlands were darkened in shadow. A strong breeze bore the first chill of the approaching night. His long hair, strung with feathers, flapped in the wind like the flames of a cold black fire, and the wind caressed his nakedness, urging him to go.

He saw something on the mat that hadn't been there a few minutes ago. It was a bow, and beside it a sheath of arrows. He looked around again. He was alone. He picked it up and tested it. He hadn't held one since he was a kid. It felt good. He looked around the desert again. There was no sign of whoever had left it. Perhaps it was the woman from the village.

Billy Two bent and emptied the urn, stamping his bare foot on the coals, pushing them under the sand to extinguish them. He felt no pain. He wrapped his gun, the knife, the urn and the bow and arrows in the mat, tied it and hoisted it over his shoulder. Barefoot and naked, Billy Two walked east.

THE DON CESAR HOTEL was called "Big Pink" because it had been stuccoed that color years before. The huge, opulent building had been restored to its magnificent turn-of-the-century elegance in the Passe-a-grille area of St. Petersburg Beach. It was now considered a chic place to dine.

Behind it, where the earth ended at the Gulf of Mexico, the setting sun had turned the water flamingo peach. All in all it looked like a postcard view of paradise.

Barrabas got out of the taxi, strode up the front steps through the luxurious lobby and straight to the doors of the dining room. He saw who he wanted. He was hard to miss. Jessup was sitting at a table against a far wall. A stern maître d' suddenly blocked his progress. He wore a big silver saucer around his neck and his nose floated so high in the air Barrabas wondered how he could see.

"You have a reservation, sir?"

Barrabas wanted to show the guy his fist and say, "Yeah, right here." But that kind of communication inevitably caused problems.

"I'm meeting my friend. Over there."

"Ah, yes. Mr. Jessup. He's expecting you. Come this way, sir."

At the table Jessup was doing what he liked to do best. Eat.

"Nile," the big Texan said magnanimously, popping a canapé into his mouth. "The specialty of the house is the Duck à l'Orange. The best on the Eastern Seaboard.

You'll love it." He turned to the maître d' as Barrabas sat in the proffered chair. "We'll have two. And the Dellac Chablis '53 to go with it."

"An excellent choice for the wine, sir," the maître d' oozed. "May I also suggest a fine sauterne for the soup course."

"May I recommend you buzz off immediately," Barrabas said impatiently, looking the lackey squarely in the face.

"No, that's fine for now," Jessup said to the man apologetically.

The maître d' buzzed off, his nose two inches higher than before.

"Nile, that was quite unnecessary," Jessup said sanctimoniously.

"So's this," Barrabas motioned at the dining room.

"Nile, I have what you need. More than you expected, probably. We'll discuss it. All will be said and done, and quickly, too. But man cannot live by war alone. He must also eat. And as I said, the Don Cesar serves the best Duck à l'Orange on the Eastern Seaboard. How could I resist when I was in the neighborhood?"

"I don't know, Jessup. Funny thing, but when I've got a problem I lose my appetite."

"I knew there had to be an explanation."

"For what?"

"Well, every time we meet it's in a car or in some little tavern where barely edible material with only a remote resemblance to food is served by long-legged cockroaches."

Barrabas watched Jessup balance a large pat of butter on a small piece of bread and pop it into his mouth.

"So, what have you got?"

Jessup chewed hard and shook his head slowly. "Nile, I don't know how you get yourself tangled up with these characters, but this time you've found yourself a real interesting crew. And let me tell you, you owe me for this one."

"Why don't you just tell me. Period."

Jessup reached down for his briefcase. He drew out a file, spread it on the table and started to read.

"Robert Braun, or Bob Braun. Retired Major, U.S. Army." Jessup looked up at Barrabas. "We do get some bad apples in the forces from time to time."

"Go on."

"Brown started his army career training Cubans for the Bay of Pigs fiasco. He worked for a while on domestic undercover projects then went back into the Army where he took up command in the Me Doc area in Vietnam. In fact, he was working with a joint CIA/ MAC special-operations group, which included teaming up with the Phoenix assassination program. He was removed from duty because of certain unexplainable atrocities that took place in areas under his command. No one could pin anything on him, though, and a young lieutenant took the blame. From there, Braun quit the Army and did what certain other Vietnam vets did. He became a mercenary."

Barrabas nodded. "That's when I met him. Angola in 1978."

"He was never fully involved in action there. Mostly he worked as a recruiter, but I understand from my sources that he used to make field inspections. Anyway, a few years back he got some money from somewhere and started up a magazine called *Torch It!* It passes on information on armaments and defense tactics and mercenary opportunities, along with a hard-line editorial policy that advocates concentration camps for most of our ethnic minorities.''

"And the gas chambers aren't far behind."

"Nope, not far, if Braun had his way with the world. The other two men with him today were probably Bill Zetmer and George Hampton. Those are their current names. There have been others. Zetmer also came out of the Phoenix assassination program in Nam and went into mercenary work. He had a reputation in Rhodesia as a cold-blooded killer. Specialized in executions, a skill he probably picked up from Phoenix. Apparently he's been running something down in Central America lately. Don't know what, but it keeps him busy."

"And the other guy. Hampton. Who's he?"

"Braun and Zetmer are brain. Hampton is brawn. A big stupid guy who answered one of the private-army ads in *Torch It!* a few years back. He was far too young for Nam and too bad for America in peacetime. So he saw his action in Africa and developed a reputation for being kind of kinky."

"Kinky? How?"

"He loves booby traps. Apparently he's an idiot in most respects but brilliant in that one. Some of his methods have already found their ways into official training manuals in several countries."

"Nothing like a good idea whose time has come."

"That's what our boys seem to think. Hampton also has a reputation for brute force as a persuasive technique. But Zetmer, he's the real expert."

"At persuasion?"

"Right. Trained at the knee of the master himself."

"Have you read the material in the briefing box I gave you yesterday?"

"No."

"Read it. You'll be interested. The master is Colonel D., who at this very moment is rotting in a Cuban prison. Apparently Zetmer was the one who gave him the nickname when he was on some kind of intelligence stint down there. And Zetmer still has a lot of admiration for his old teacher."

"Is that it?"

Jessup shook his head. "Nope. There's a few more hangers-on, other characters who are basically run-of-the-mill mercs and part of Braun's little circle. They call themselves 'X Command,' by the way, and they have a headquarters. A little beach house out on Anna Maria Island, a sandbar about forty miles south of here."

"Sounds like these boys are financed."

"That's where I drew a blank. If so, by whom is a big question. Now maybe they got their own money. Maybe they borrow it from their mothers. Who knows? But they do get money from somewhere. And probably have an arsenal to equal that of the Florida National Guard."

"But none of this answers the sixty-four-million-dollar question."

"What's that?"

"Typical, Jessup. You immerse yourself in details and forget how we got here in the first place. What do these guys want with Tony Lopez?"

Jessup looked across the table at Barrabas. He had no answer.

At that moment, the maître d' appeared, ice bucket and stand in one hand and bottle in the other.

"The Dellac Chablis '53," he said with flair, opening the cork with professional flourish. He poured some into the silver saucer around his neck and tasted it.

"Ah, yes. A rare wine. Only our most discerning customers order it." He arced the bottle through the air and poured some into Jessup's glass. He gave Barrabas a condescending glance down the side of his nose as he poured.

Jessup sipped, swished and swallowed. "Excellent."

The maître d' filled the glass.

Barrabas stood up and shuffled Jessup's file together. "I won't be eating. I've got work to do." He put the file under his arm and turned to go.

"Are you certain you do not wish to share in the opening of this unusual wine, sir?" the maître d' simpered.

Barrabas turned back to the table. "Sure," he said. He grabbed the bottle from the maître d' and stuck it between his lips, guzzling back a mouthful. He held it there a few seconds. He seemed to be thinking about it. He looked at the surprised waiter and nodded, his cheeks ballooned from the wine. He swallowed. "Great stuff."

Jessup buried his face in his hands in embarrassment. "Oh Barrabas," he moaned. The waiter was apoplectic. Barrabas slammed the bottle down on the table and left.

He looked back at the Big Pink as he went down the front steps and hailed a cab. It was a nice hotel and he'd already heard about its cuisine and its legendary wine cellars, the best in Florida. It would be a nice place to take Erika if they were ever down this way on a jaunt. For dinner some night. The maître d's night off.

9

The senator sat in his wheelchair in the walnut-paneled study of his Georgetown house, contemplating Miss Roseline through the glass doors that led to the garden. He had sent her out there to cut some flowers, an excuse to watch her bend over the lower shrubs as she clipped and gathered blossoms. Watching Miss Roseline was a joy. Dealing with her was a pain. She was quite unlike any of the others in the long line of women that had passed through the senator's employ—and through his pawing hands. She took care of his needs, such as they were. Life in a wheelchair had limited his expression in certain regards. He would never forgive Jeremiah or Nile Barrabas for putting him there. Jeremiah, the mad dictator, was dead. With luck, soon Barrabas would be, too.

There was a knock on the door.

"Come in!" he shouted sharply, disturbed from his contemplation of Miss Roseline's shapely posterior.

A servant entered. "The gentleman you expected is here, Senator."

"Well, show him in!"

Swiftly and silently the servant disappeared. A few seconds later the senator's mysterious visitor appeared. His hair was carefully coiffed and his suit expensive. He walked with the easy gait of a wealthy man. The smile on his face contrasted sharply with the senator's scowl.

"Cheer up, Senator. Things are not as bad as they seem," the visitor said, throwing himself down into an armchair near the old politician. He crossed his legs and pulled out a gold cigarette case.

"Fine for you to say," the senator muttered. "You're not in a wheelchair." He pressed the button on the arm and the chair wheeled across the floor to come to a stop a hand's length from the man's knee. The man drew a cigarette from his case and nonchalantly tapped it on his knee.

"Tsk, tsk. So bitter. You waste a lot of energy with your obsession."

"My obsession? I thought you shared my goal."

"Of course I do." The man stuck the cigarette in his mouth and lit it with a diamond-studded gold lighter. "I share it. But not for the same reasons, obviously. Barrabas himself means nothing. Except that he's dangerous. And in the way. In a war such as this one, such people should be eliminated. That's all. You lust for revenge. For me, it's a practical matter. Business, as it were."

"And is our business booming?" the senator asked sarcastically.

"Booming! Ha ha. Yes, I suppose it is." He blew a long stream of smoke in the senator's direction. It hovered like a cloud around the senator's head. The politician waved his hand to disperse it.

"Then tell me!"

"So impatient." The visitor sighed, enjoying the senator's fury. "You have no idea how much this operation is costing me, do you?"

"And I don't particularly care, either."

"No, I suppose not. As long as your check arrives on time."

"Can't we get down to business? Have we no sense of urgency? If I could move from this wheelchair I'd . . ."

"You'd what, Senator? Strangle me? I can see it in your eyes. A most imprudent move. I'm really not worth a life sentence. No one is."

"Then let's talk about a death sentence. Barrabas's."

"We have the boy," the man said abruptly, flicking his cigarette over an ashtray. "Soon the SOBs will follow X Command to Cuba where they will free our dear friend Colonel D. from his Cuban prison cell. Then we will reverse the trap. The proper files have been slipped to Walker Jessup who is now in Florida revealing their contents to Nile Barrabas."

The senator wrung his hands in anticipation. Then he broke into a cracked smile. "Excellent," he mused. He manipulated the buttons on his chair and the motor whirred him away from the visitor.

The slippery senator slid to a stop behind his desk and looked across at the man in the expensive suit. At that moment the French doors from the garden opened and Miss Roseline stepped into the room.

Both men looked around.

"Am I interrupting?" she asked.

"Not at all, Miss Roseline. We were just finished."

"You were saying, Senator?" the visitor asked.

The senator looked at him. "Ah yes. It's a brilliant strategy. The current project, that is. The pursuers, unbeknownst to them, will, in fact, be the pursued." He laughed, relishing the idea.

The visitor took a long, relaxed drag on his cigarette. Miss Roseline quietly eyed the thin man, then the senator's smile.

10

Night had fallen when the taxi deposited Nile Barrabas outside the gates of the SOBs' oceanfront estate. The long street was illuminated by the yellow glow of the incandescent street lighting, which threw the deep green shrubs and trees into eerie plastic relief. He crossed the sidewalk to the gates, which now were closed.

Nate Beck emerged from the shadows on the other side with a soft rustle of leaves. He wore dark clothing and carried an M-16. They weren't taking any chances now.

"Hey, Colonel." He greeted the tall, white-haired warrior quietly and unwrapped the chain to open the high iron gates from the inside. "O'Toole just got in. He's at the house."

Barrabas nodded and slipped through the opening, pushing the gate closed behind him. Beck started to lock it up again.

"I got what I needed, Nate." Barrabas held up the file Jessup had brought. "I'll send someone down to relieve you in half an hour. Then I'll fill you in."

"I'll be waiting," said Beck. He moved back into the shadows again. Barrabas headed up the driveway to the house.

It was lit up like a Christmas tree and the lights from the big windows that ran around the house spilled out across the lawns. Outside the big front doors, Liam O'Toole, the red-haired Irish-American who served as the colonel's second-in-command, paced back and forth around Nanos's T-bird. Barrabas could hear Nanos's loud voice.

"I tell you, Liam. This is what happens when you lend your car to your best friend. He takes it out. It gets wrecked."

O'Toole stopped by the front fender and stuck his finger into one of the bullet holes that perforated the black metal. "Looks like they mean business, whoever they are."

"Sure they do. That's it. It's never anyone's fault that it gets wrecked. It just happens. But it always happens when someone else takes it out for a drive."

Barrabas couldn't help smiling as he heard the Greek's complaining. The man was obsessive. About cars, about women. And about war. Sometimes Nanos was a pain in the ass. But he was a helluva fighter, and underneath the bitching and the boasting there was a good man.

O'Toole saw Barrabas first.

"Colonel!" he greeted him. They shook hands.

"Hey, Colonel." Nanos finally turned from the car. "The tires are replaced and I had the engine and cooling system checked out for damage. The bullets nicked the engine block, broke the distributor cap and KO'd the windshield-washer container. But she's fixed and ready to go, in top form," he said enthusiastically. "Except for the hubcaps," he added forlornly.

"Good. Looks like we're going to need it tonight."

The mercs went inside the house.

Claude Hayes was in the living room where mags of

5.56mm bullets were counted out on the floor. He was centered between two piles of M-16s, the paratrooper's model with the folding stocks. He gave a rifle from one pile the once-over and put it in the second.

He looked up when his fellow fighters filed in.

"Claude, get the map of Florida laid out. We're going out for a drive," Barrabas ordered. He pulled a chair out from the table and flipped through Jessup's file.

A few minutes later the men were briefed and they were looking at a map of the west coast of Florida. Anna Maria Island was a key, not much more than a sandbar with palm trees and houses forty miles south of Tampa. It was seven miles long and half a mile wide, separated from the mainland by another half mile of water. Three causeways led across the island to the mainland. There were three small communities on the island. Anna Maria Holmes Beach was at the north, Bradenton Beach at the southern tip and Anna Maria Key at the center. Both sides of the narrow channel that separated the island from the mainland were sprinkled with marinas.

"There," said Barrabas, placing his finger squarely on Bradenton Beach. "X Command has a beach house so it must be here along the gulf side. We'll find it when we get there."

"When do we leave, Colonel?" Liam asked.

"Now." Barrabas started folding the map. "Claude, put the weapons in the trunk of the car. Alex, you go down and relieve Nate so I can brief him on what we're doing. Liam, did you bring us something to wear?"

The ex-Army sergeant nodded. "Black combat pants

and sweaters. Nanos and I picked up some face paint on the way in from the airport.''

"Okay, let's get dressed. Be out in ten minutes."

Hayes picked his M-16 off the table and stood. "Colonel?" he said slowly. "You got any idea what these guys want with Tony Lopez?"

Barrabas shook his head. "But be prepared for anything," he warned.

Hayes nodded slowly, not looking at any of them. He appeared to be looking over their heads through the darkness outside at the ocean. "Don't look now," he said, "but someone's creeping around in front of the house."

"Shit," Barrabas swore softly. "How the fuck did they get past Beck?"

The mercs kept silent, each man tensing. They stood up calmly and moved away from the table, out of view of the wide windows. Hayes and O'Toole headed toward the hallway. All of them had one thought beyond the danger. What had happened to Nate Beck?

Barrabas and Nanos stood against a wall. Barrabas reached out his arm to the light switch and flicked it off. The room dimmed, lit now only by light coming in from the hallway. He drew his handgun from his shoulder holster and crawled below the windowsill until he came to glass doors that led outside. Nanos followed.

"Go!" The colonel gave his order. With his foot high, he kicked the door open and crouched low. The door crashed backward and slammed. The sound of breaking windowpanes shattered the night. Both mercs spun out the door guns up and ready to blow.

The terrace and the lawns were empty.

"Cover it here," Barrabas snapped at Nanos.

He pushed away from the house and circled to the left, disappearing around the corner.

Nanos backed into the darkness under the overhanging eaves and kept down. He heard footsteps coming from the other direction. He tensed and saw a man sidle quickly around the other corner of the house and dart behind a stand of palm trees. He could recognize the shape in the darkness. It was O'Toole.

He waited a moment until the Irishman darted again from the palm trees along the back of the house.

"O'Toole," he called in a loud whisper.

The red-haired man looked in his direction. "See anything?"

"Uh-uh. You?"

"Nothing."

O'Toole came to his side. Both men looked back and forth anxiously along the grounds and down to the beach. In the dimly reflected light from the ocean they could make out no movement.

"Let's go back in," said O'Toole. "Maybe it's a false alarm. We should check on Beck, though."

The two mercs went back inside through the shattered glass doors.

"There goes our damage deposit," Nanos cracked, reaching for the light switch. He flicked it on just as Barrabas and Hayes entered from the hallway.

When the lights went on, the mercs stared, speechless.

The intruder was sitting on a chair at the table, studying the map of Anna Maria Island.

It was Billy Two.

Dressed to kill.

He wore a black sleeveless T-shirt, black fatigue pants and high laced-up jackboots. His long black hair was pulled back from his forehead with a beaded headband and decorated with feathers. His face and arms were blackened by camouflage makeup. Across each cheek were diagonal streaks of red and blue stripes. His thick biceps and wrists were girdled by leather arm bands. The one around his left wrist held a knife. And the blue and red stripes continued on the outside of his arms. Osage war paint. Every time the SOBs saw him, Billy Two was reaching further back to the time of his warrior forebearers. Way back. This time, on the table beside him, lay a long bow and some arrows. Billy looked up at his surprised companions.

"Beck's down at the front gate," he said matter-of-factly. "I saw him on the way in. He doesn't know I'm here."

"How the hell did you get past him?" Nanos demanded.

Billy Two shrugged and studied the map.

"I'm not even going to ask." Barrabas grinned. "It's good to have you here, Billy Two."

AN HOUR LATER the six men coasted down the Gulf Coast Highway, squeezed three to a seat in the T-bird. The trunk was full of guns and ammunition.

The land they drove through was pure Florida, a long, continuous stretch of suburban-resort development and shopping centers interspersed among tracts of citrus orchards. The signs betrayed Florida's sun culture with names like "Frodo's Fruitland" and "Palmtree Paradise Trailer Park."

For most of the way the mercs rode in silence with the roof up and the windows down, the hot summer winds flattening their faces. Nanos drove fast.

Once Beck turned the radio on and tried to dial in some music. It was on-the-hour newscast time and the lead reports were about some terrorist activity at Tampa airport that morning, some freeway maniacs sought for dangerous driving, and a mother and her two sons who had been slaughtered in their suburban home.

"At least we didn't do the number on them," Hayes commented slowly from the back seat.

Barrabas turned the radio off.

"No, but if the cops stop us now with our trunk full of guns, they'll probably pin it on us."

Nanos glanced up into the mirror as he drove to look at Billy Two in the back seat. "Billy, I'd still like to know how you got past our security."

Billy Two answered slowly. There always seemed to be a dreamlike quality to his words now. "Do your electronics stop the night?" he asked. "If I become the night, then I also cannot be stopped."

"Cut the mystic rap, man. How'd you do it?"

"I'll show you sometime, Alex. When your spirit force is ready to guide you."

"Billy, don't take offense, old buddy, but..." Nanos turned to Barrabas. "Colonel, are you sure he isn't dangerous?"

"If he can do tricks like the one tonight, he's on our side," Barrabas said.

O'Toole spoke up. "What I want to know is what he plans on doing with the bow and arrow."

"Watch me," Billy Two said evenly.

At the city of Bradenton, on the mainland, Nanos turned the car left through an intersection cornered by shopping plazas and headed for the causeway that led across to Bradenton Beach on Anna Maria Island. The land was flat and wilder, the houses smaller. There was a thin edge of marshland along the coast, with marinas and boat-repair yards on both sides of the highway just before the causeway.

Across the channel of water, lights floated, marking the outlines of more marinas and bridges to the north and south. Anna Maria Island came into view as a dark line at the end of the road, stretching off in both directions and fringed with palm trees.

A great, modern, ramshackle hotel studded with cocktail lounges in a rustic beach-house style glowed with lights on one side of the highway. It was 10:00 P.M. and the lounge set was still coming and going.

At the end of the causeway, Nanos took the car up an incline onto the island and past a forest of pine trees. The road ended in a T at the highway that ran up and down the seven-mile length of Anna Maria. Beyond the road the whitecapped waves of the gulf washed up on a long stretch of public beach.

"Turn right," Barrabas ordered. Nanos did as he was instructed, while the colonel looked carefully at the buildings and houses they passed, searching for a number or sign to tell them where they were in relation to X Command's beach-house headquarters. The two-lane highway was busy with Saturday-night traffic heading to the hotels and restaurants on the southern part of the island. The T-bird was indistinguishable from the variety of expensive cars that went by.

Barrabas snapped on the map light above the glove compartment and bent over the folded highway map. "There's another public beach and a forested stretch about a mile up the road. The beach house should be right near there. We'll look for a place to park and go in on foot.''

"There sure isn't much space to hide an assault operation on this sandbar,'' O'Toole commented.

After a few minutes of twisting and turning down the narrow, curving road, Nanos found the long entrance gate to the beachfront park and drove through. The red taillights of a half-dozen cars glowed in the parking lot. Lovers' Lane.

"Try the far end, down by the forest,'' Barrabas said. Nanos took the T-bird farther down the beach to where the little forest of carefully planted pines grew in neat rows. He turned the car so the rear wheels and trunk were in the darkness of the forest. He killed the lights and engine.

"Get yourselves ready. I'll find out where we're going.'' Barrabas got out of the car and pulled a tweed jacket from the back seat. He put it on over his black shirt and shoulder holster and walked back across the beach to the main road.

He sauntered along slowly, like a man out for a stroll. The numbers of the houses that fronted the highway suggested that X Command's beach house was close by and on the ocean side of the highway. Barrabas walked past the pine forest that fronted the road, which swerved abruptly right, following the coastline of the island. Between the edge of the pine forest and the road was a large two-story frame house. Like all the new dwellings on Anna Maria, it was built on stilts. The second story was the main floor, and there was room underneath for cars to park. A closed-in stairwell led to the upper deck, which ran around three sides of the house. There were no cars and no lights on inside. The nouse number was marked on one of the little stone pillars that formed the front gate. This was it.

The night was calm, moonless, and the only noises were the slow wash of the waves on the beach and Barrabas's boots crunching on the gravel shoulder of the highway. He carefully surveyed the house and adjacent surroundings. The road led off along the coast past another forested stretch. Across the road was a church, its windows as dark as the X Command house. The nearest lights came from some buildings almost half a mile farther up the road. Twice cars swept by, the voices of rowdy teenagers trailing on the air as they passed.

A night made for an assault. The SOBs would have the same advantages of privacy that the beach house afforded its owners. It was quiet and deserted. Any noises—the quick bursts of autofire and the slamming of a door or window, the shouts of the fight—would be scattered and distorted by the strong breezes blowing in off the gulf.

When Barrabas got back to the waiting mercs they were dressed in black, their faces smeared, companions of the night.

"Either no one's home or else it's a trap of some kind," he told them.

"Or both," O'Toole added.

"Right. Beware of electronic surveillance devices."

Hayes turned the key in the trunk and the lid sprang up. The stunted M-16s, their stocks folded in, glistened dully on the felt carpet. The mercs reached in and hauled out their weapons along with enough 20-round mags to last and a few extra just in case. Beck handed out silencers, and the mercs quickly screwed the metal cylinders onto the barrels. They were ready.

Beck and O'Toole took the long way around, walking to the beach to cut around the pine forest and approach the house from the water. Beck and Starfoot went through the forest. Barrabas and Nanos took the car. They drove around to the front gate and parked by the road.

"Now what?" Nanos asked when he and the colonel reached the gates.

"I go in and knock and see if anyone's home. You wait here and cover me if someone comes. Or goes."

The two mercs slipped into the driveway. Nanos disappeared toward the forest. Barrabas eyed the high, dark house. He didn't like the feel of it at all.

By the time he got to the door, Billy Two and Nate Beck were waiting for him underneath the house. Barrabas felt something brush against his leg. Two glowing topaz eyes looked up at him. A cat. It meowed and rubbed against his legs again.

"Colonel," Billy Two whispered in the darkness, "with your okay, I can shimmy up a post and climb onto the deck."

Barrabas nodded. "Be careful. Feel around for security devices," he whispered. "Razor blades and electric wires." Billy Two padded off to one of the corner posts. Barrabas noticed that the Indian had no boots on. A moment later Starfoot had gripped the large round post with his arms and legs and was pulling himself up to the overhead floor beams.

Barrabas and Nate Beck stood on either side of the door with their backs to the wall. Barrabas tightened his grip on the autorifle in his right hand, holding it like a handgun, and reached out with his left to try the handle.

It turned. He held it as far clockwise as it would go

and took a deep breath, visualizing quickly his next step. Push the door open, go in low with a finger tightening on the trigger, ready to blow away anyone who looked dangerous.

Headlights on the road approached and the sound of a car engine grew louder. He waited until it passed, his fingers resting lightly around the doorknob. The car went by. But the cat beat him to it.

The little animal jumped up, putting its two front paws against the bottom panel of the door.

Surprised by the unexpected movement, Barrabas's light grip slipped and the door swung back.

Boom!

The upper lintel of the door blew up, throwing jagged splinters of 2x4 outward in a cloud of smoke and smaller debris. With a terrified meow, the cat sprang back through the booby-trapped doorway and fled into the darkness. The door, blown from its top hinge, careened for a few seconds before falling outward at a mad angle and banging against the shattered frame.

Upstairs, a glass window was smashed.

Barrabas felt a sharp sting on his face as he spun away from the explosion. His hand came away from his cheek warm and sticky. A splinter. He and Beck breathed in relief. If the cat hadn't gone first, the explosion would have taken their heads off.

"Colonel, there's a prissfour in the car."

"Get it."

Beck ran quickly for the gate. The prissfour, or PRS4, was an explosives detector.

Barrabas heard the soft pad of human footsteps on the stairs. He looked through the clearing dust and smoke.

"Ouch!" Billy Two swore. He stood halfway down the steps from the upper deck, bending over to pull a splinter from his bare foot. He tugged it out and looked down at the colonel. "No one's home," he said.

"Billy Two, don't move an inch," Barrabas snapped quickly. "Those stairs could be mined." He took his flashlight from his belt and flicked it on, directing the beam up and down the steps. Billy Two swallowed and stood perfectly still.

The lower steps on the inside were covered with debris. Barrabas went around the wooden stairwell to the back and shone his light on the underside of the steps. They were clear.

He moved back to the door in time to greet O'Toole, Hayes and Beck, who carried the explosive detector.

"Nanos will stay at the gate," said Beck.

Barrabas nodded. "Okay, Billy, the steps are clear."

"What in hell happened here?" O'Toole asked, looking at the shattered doorway. "Pull firing device with a charge over the upper doorjamb," he answered himself.

"You should know," Barrabas said. "You're the expert on demolitions. Where do you figure the next one will be?"

"Where we least expect it," O'Toole answered curtly.

"Let's go upstairs," the colonel instructed.

Billy Two had already gone back up and was waiting for them at the top.

"Colonel, while you were blowing up the doorway, I smashed the glass door at the front and went inside. If there's anyone there they're back in the bedrooms or something. The living room is clear."

"O'Toole, you want to brief them on what not to do once we get inside. Beck, you start where Billy Two broke the window and check the floor so we know where to walk.'' Barrabas eyed the front door, which led off the deck, and pulled his knife from the belt sheath. ''I'll check this one out.''

''Basically, it's simple,'' said O'Toole. ''Walk where Beck tells you you can walk. Don't sit anywhere, lie anywhere, touch anything or turn anything on. Keep your eyes peeled—and I mean peeled—for low-lying wires strung between the legs of furniture or between doorjambs. But whoever set this place up isn't likely to be that obvious. Just remember, don't touch anything. Not even a book or an ashtray.''

The red-haired Irish-American joined Barrabas by the front door. He already had the molding around the inside of the doorframe pried up and was pulling the last strip off.

''You want me to do it, Colonel?'' O'Toole offered.

Neither of them wore protective gear and both knew what a little bit of TNT could do to a man.

''Nice of you to offer, Liam. But I can use the practice.''

Barrabas rolled up his sleeves. The job was exacting. He took a thin, stiff wire from the pocket of his fatigues and, starting at the bottom left-hand corner, inserted it between the door and the frame. Slowly, almost imperceptibly, he raised it upward, focusing his concentration on the feel of the wire between his thumb and index finger. Halfway up the door he felt the wire stop. There was something there and it wasn't the latch.

''Side-jamb rigging,'' O'Toole muttered under his breath. ''Colonel, they've got a clever boy to do all this.''

"We have to dismantle it from the inside," Barrabas said. "Let's get in the same way Billy Two did."

At the front of the house the glass door had been smashed open. It was barely large enough for the muscled mercs to step through without catching their clothing on the jagged edges. Inside, Billy Two and Hayes aimed their flashlights in a cross beam to guide Nate, who moved the prissfour slowly around the carpet.

"Floor looks clear," Nate said. "But I haven't tried the furniture."

"Don't anyone touch the front door," Barrabas warned. "Or you'll lose your crotch."

"Colonel," O'Toole called from behind him, "look at this." Barrabas turned. O'Toole had pulled the curtains aside from the sliding doors. Another explosive device was screwed to the inside frame. Open the door, slide it back, and the frame hits a pressure firing device.

"They didn't want us in here, did they?" Billy Two said.

"Too bad," said Barrabas. "We're in." Something was bothering him. Not checking out the door downstairs was a dumb mistake. Very dumb. Especially when it had been clearly noted in the briefing on X Command that one of their operatives was an expert in booby traps.

But that wasn't all that bothered him. The traps were in all the obvious places. Too obvious for an expert. It was a better strategy to let them get inside and then blow them up. Which left a big question. What was waiting for them next?

Beck and Hayes disappeared into a hallway that led farther into the house. Barrabas looked around. All of

them were uneasy, keeping their feet planted in one spot
and not willing to move any more than they had to.

The house was modern and expensively furnished,
and bore little resemblance to any kind of a commando
headquarters. A metal fireplace stood against one wall
with plush leather sofas on either side. There was no
sign of military hardware of any kind. It was a resort
house, nothing more.

Nate called from the back of the house, and Barrabas
went to the door off the corridor.

"The hallway's okay, Colonel," Beck said as Hayes
stuck his head from a doorway and added, "Come and
have a look at this."

A bedroom had been converted into a command center. The window looked out over the ocean. Maps of the
Caribbean and Florida lined the walls. One detailed the
Cuban coastline. Barrabas noticed almost immediately
a small red circle a hundred miles down the coast from
Havana. Along another wall, a long desk stretched from
one end to the other. A number of notebooks were piled
near some files. On the other side was a large shortwave
radio. Earphones lay by the control panel, and a tiny
red light indicated the power was on.

Beck passed the detector over the books and files.

"This is it," said Hayes.

"Are the books okay?" Barrabas asked.

Beck nodded, putting down the scope on the detector.
Barrabas picked up a book and flipped through it. It
was a log written in code. Each page was a mass of
handwritten numbers grouped in long columns.

"Beck, take a look at this."

He glanced over the pages. Nate had been a cryptog-
rapher during his stint with the U.S. Army. His codes

were now used by some of the country's intelligence services.

"Can you decode it?" Barrabas asked.

Beck nodded. "You bet, Colonel. It's one of mine." He took another book from the table. "Sort of," he added. "It looks like a variation on a system I originated. I can run it through the computer when we get back to the house. I know the intelligence agencies ripped off a few of the codes I put together for the Army. These guys used to have connections. Looks like they brought the codes with them. It'll only take me a few minutes to figure them out."

"Let's take all this stuff and get out of here," Barrabas told the mercenaries. "And bring that map of Cuba up there."

"Colonel." Hayes pointed to the corner of the room. Beck recognized it. Barrabas didn't. "It's the knapsack Tony Lopez had with him when he came to visit us," Hayes told his commander.

"Bring it, too," Barrabas said. He started to move from the room.

Hayes shone his flashlight over the shortwave radio.

"This is still set to one of the marine channels. Why don't we see what's on the airwaves?" He picked up the earphones and put them on. There was no sound. He turned the volume up. Still nothing. Then he noticed the earphones weren't plugged in.

He picked up the jack and aimed it for the proper hole when Barrabas's big hand came out and grabbed his. The headset was ripped from his head.

"Beck, bring the prissfour here," Barrabas ordered.

The electronics expert lowered the scope of the detector along the headset. The needle soared.

Barrabas slowly unscrewed the earpiece. The diaphragm had been removed and was filled with a dark, powdered explosive. He shook some out onto the desk. Underneath was a tiny electronic detonator.

"That would give you quite a headache," Beck commented wryly.

"Uh-uh. No headache at all," said Hayes.

"No head." Barrabas scraped the explosive back into the earpiece and screwed it back together. "Maybe whoever left it that way will forget about it by the time they get back." He left the earphones on the control board.

The place was creepy.

"Let's take what we need and get out," he told his men.

11

Little more than an hour later, the SOBs were back at the house near Tampa. Nate Beck immediately went to the keyboard of his portable computer. Soon he was flipping through pages in the notebooks they'd found at the beach house and keyboarding data into his machine. He was oblivious to everything else around him.

Nanos and O'Toole went off in the T-bird to find food. No one had eaten since early morning. The excitement took the edge off appetites. But now, with a lull in the action, hunger caught up with them.

Barrabas sat in a padded lawn chair on the terrace behind the house, facing the Gulf of Mexico and watching the waves crash onto the beach. Slightly to the north, the lights of St. Petersburg glimmered along the edge of Tampa Bay. In his lap lay the wine-colored folder Jessup had given him in New York the day before. The briefing papers on Colonel D. He hadn't even opened it yet.

There was something missing, he thought. Something or someone. Or maybe not. Maybe he was looking at it all but seeing only the tip. Or the top fin. Whatever was submerged was deadly. He was sure of that.

All he had to do was put the pieces together. Or look at what he had and recognize the shape of it. Easier said than done.

The real mystery was Tony Lopez. What did Tony want? He wanted to meet the buddies of the older brother he idolized. It was likely that Tony had just stumbled into something by accident. If that was so, what had he stumbled into? That depended on what X Command wanted him for. Bait. Bait for what? For Barrabas and the SOBs.

If Tony was the bait and the mercs were the quarry, what was the trap?

Barrabas listened to the soothing roar of the waves on the beach and watched the fluttering glimmer of the lights around Tampa Bay. The sixty-five-foot cruiser bobbed gently on the surface of the water a few hundred yards out.

Colonel D. Somehow the Latin American torture master sitting in his prison cell in an old Cuban fortress was the key to this. He was convinced of it the moment the thought entered his mind. Convinced firmly.

Someone very powerful in Washington had been at Barrabas, via the Fixer, to take the assignment on Colonel D. Later it turns out that one of X Command had been a student of the infamous colonel's. Barrabas didn't believe in coincidence. And despite Billy Two's recent behavior, he didn't believe in hocus-pocus, either. Colonel D. didn't just pop into his life from two different directions in one day. It had the makings of a scheme.

And he had found something to confirm it: the Caribbean map they had taken from the wall of the beach house on Anna Maria. A tiny circle had been drawn in ink at a nameless spot on the coast of Cuba. Barrabas knew what it marked. The Sangrino Prison.

Barrabas felt a chill ripple up and down his spine.

Colonel D. didn't frighten him. Nor did the relatively straightforward mission of going into Cuba and offing him. It was all in his line of work.

But if a trap was being set and Colonel D. was the lure, then the trap was being set in Washington, not by X Command. The man with the gun was pointing it in his direction.

THE SOUND OF THE KEY in the rusty door and the screech of ancient hinges abruptly awakened Colonel D. from a deep sleep. He was momentarily disoriented. Then he remembered where he was. The Sangrino Prison. The man from Havana had finally come, earlier that day, and once again the colonel had fallen into a deep sleep before their little chat had ended. Now the man was gone, and he was still groggy from the terrible sedatives they'd given him.

The door of his cell swung slowly inward. The colonel waited. Perhaps his sole visitor would return. But no one entered. After what seemed like a long time, he sat up and swung his legs off his bed onto the floor. Silence. There was no one there.

Puzzled, the colonel leaned forward off the bed and peered around the door out into the corridor. It was deserted.

Stranger and stranger, thought the colonel.

He stood and walked to the open doorway where he looked up and down the dim corridor in both directions. The stone walls of the ancient building were dank with moisture and glistened with lime deposits from corroding stone. The corridor was lit by fading yellow bulbs set at intervals along the walls in little wire cages. The colonel stepped from his cell and walked down the corridor.

He listened carefully for sounds of the guards, but heard only the slow trickle of water on the stones and the soft-shoe dance of rats. Then he heard, very faintly and from very far away a sound that sent chills up and down his spine. It was unmistakable—the perfect elegance of baroque string music, as if a chamber ensemble was holding concert in a room in the prison. The colonel recognized the music. He had used it many times. It was his favorite.

As his victims twisted and writhed in pain and agony, straining at their bonds as if they might fly from their bodies to avoid the physical hell they had been plunged into, as their eyes bulged from their heads and screams tore from their mouths, they heard the delicately peaceful strains of violins and clarinets and the soft, smooth voice of the Torture Master asking questions.

The colonel steadied himself. The music grew louder. It was beckoning him. He walked slowly down the corridor. He was covered with sweat, and salty beads dripped into his eyes. He wiped his face with the palm of his hand. The music was coming from behind a door at the end of the corridor.

He put out his hand to open it, but before he touched the rusting metal handle it swung sharply back and clunked heavily against the stone wall. Music poured into the corridor riding on beams of searing white light. The colonel's hand flew to his face to shield his eyes. Gradually they adjusted, a little. He peered against the painful brilliance with the flat of his hand raised to his brow. Gradually the room became discernible.

He recognized it immediately. It was his torture chamber. Or rather, one of his design, like the ones he had built in prisons and palaces throughout the Americas.

The floors and walls were gleaming white tile, as sanitary and pristine as a hospital operating room. In front of him was a large comfortable chair. On either side, chrome wagons held stainless-steel trays in which dozens of odd instruments lay in rows. Instruments to poke and tear and cut and pierce.

On the other side of the chair there was a large black box. Wires led from it to the wall on the other side of the room. Colonel D.'s eyes followed the wires.

They multiplied into long black tentacles and spread upward, wrapping around the body of a prisoner, bound and trussed and hanging by the arms from a hook in the ceiling. The victim's back was to the colonel, but the curves of the body, the narrow shoulders, the tiny waist, the flare of the wide hips and buttocks, indicated that it was clearly a woman. The long dark hair was wet from the bath of mineral water, which made it highly conducive to electric current.

The graceful strains of music continued their slow minuet around the room. A red light on the black box by the chair flashed. The colonel strode forward and sat at the edge of the chair, his eyes fixed on the victim who awaited his touch. He flicked the dial to forty. There was a sharp hum, and suddenly the body of the woman recoiled and jerked in spasms. A scream ripped from her body and slashed at the air. Her body flailed and swung on the rope that held her. The chorus of violins in the chamber concert swelled to a triumphant climax. The colonel let the dial drop back to zero. The torture victim stopped lurching and screaming, and slowly the body began to turn on the rope. The colonel heard laughter, as if the room had suddenly filled with an appreciative audience. He turned around.

He gasped, drawing his hand to his face.

Behind him, rows of medals gleamed across the beribboned chests of the most powerful generals and dictators of Latin America. He recognized them. He had worked for them.

They held champagne glasses.

A man in an expensive leisure suit stepped from the lines of other men. He smiled, exposing two rows of perfect teeth, and held his glass high. It was the man from the CIA. The one who had given him the name that grew notorious, the one who had first called him Colonel D.

"A toast," the man from the CIA shouted, turning to the generals and dictators standing behind him. He looked back at the colonel and raised his glass, his eyes looking over the rim and nailing hard into the colonel's. "To Colonel Death. And to his many talents." The CIA man smiled and winked at the astonished colonel. With a jerk of his head he motioned toward the hanging torture victim at the far end of the sterile room. "All your clients agree that your talents are formidable."

The colonel turned in the direction the CIA man looked as the row of generals and dictators raised their glasses and shouted over the soft music. "To Colonel D."

The rope was swinging around and with it the victim was turning to face the colonel. As the profile of the woman came into view, he felt a thud in his gut. It was too late. The victim turned to face him fully. Her eyes were wide with hatred and revulsion and pain.

It was Maria!

The colonel screamed to deny it. "Nooo!" He turned back to look at the men who had been his supporters, to plead that this was a dream, a joke, a trick, something, anything, other than truth.

The dictators and generals were gone.

They had been replaced by something else.

Something worse.

They stood in rows, covered with blood and sores, their skin marked with burns and scorched by electrodes, missing nails and eyes and tongues and limbs. They stood naked and mutilated and they looked at him and then they started to walk.

Their arms stretched in front of them, their bloodied fingers waved, inviting him forward into their ghoulish grip. The colonel screamed again, this time an incomprehensible scream of terror. He threw himself from the chair and backed away.

Too late.

"You're dead," he cried. "You're dead. I killed you. All of you!" His voice clawed through the stark white light and over the serene sound of the calming music. To no avail. The colonel's victims had returned from their graves. They encircled him and their bony hands gripped his arms and shoulders and tugged him forward. The crowd parted and pushed him at the white-tiled wall.

There was a toilet there.

The toilet was filled with excrement.

The hands that gripped the colonel's shoulders pushed him down.

He screamed.

They pushed him harder, forcing his face into the foul matter. His scream ended with a muffled splat. Colonel D. shuddered and whimpered as he began to smother.

THE MAN FROM HAVANA quickly shuffled through the papers that the prison commandant had handed him the moment he had left Colonel D.'s cell. "It all appears to be in order," Luis Castro said. "It's unfortunate that the interrogation techniques must culminate now at precisely the time when I have been ordered to remove the prisoner to Havana."

"Certainly, Captain, it is not due to any problems here at the Sangrino Prison?" said the commandant. "We have followed the regimen of sedatives you ordered with great care."

"Not at all, Commandant. The results of my interrogation, which are taking place this very moment, indicate that you have treated the prisoner with care. No, there are rumors that an attempt will be made by foreign agents to free Colonel D."

"From the Sangrino Prison! But that is preposterous."

"Nonetheless," said the man from Havana, "I have been ordered to remove the prisoner as soon as possible. And the order came from my uncle's office."

The commandant was impressed. Luis Castro's uncle was not to be disobeyed. "It should be possible to extract the necessary information from the prisoner within the next two or three hours. We can go to the cell now."

"Very good. Bring the note pads and tape recorder. I shall capture every word of information he gives us."

The captain and the commandant left the office and began a brisk walk into the bowels of the Sangrino Prison. Captain Castro curled his thin mustache with the tip of his finger as they walked. Annoyed at the gesture, he stopped. It was a habit he'd picked up from

Colonel D., a case of the torturer taking on the personality of the victim.

Captain Luis Castro was a professional interrogator. The best that Cuba had to offer. His method was slow but almost always effective. It required knowing intimately the psyche of the victim and turning that psyche against itself. For every strength there existed a weakness. It was merely a matter of turning that strength upside down. Every man had his devils. Unleash them, set them free; they would break the prisoner. And when the prisoner was broken, the torturer had only to reach out a healing hand.

As they descended the last flight of stone steps in the nether regions of the prison, a sharp, ghastly scream echoed from the depths below. Castro and the commandant exchanged glances. They walked faster until they came to the dimly lit corridor at the end of which was the colonel's cell. Several prison guards and two men in white coats waited anxiously outside the cell. One held a tray. On the tray a syringe waited.

"Captain, the subject has reached the strongest part of the hallucinatory effect. He..." One of the white-coated men motioned into the cell.

Captain Castro turned and walked in. The colonel squatted on the floor of his cell, his head hanging over the porcelain bowl of his own toilet. He sat as if invisible hands pushed his face down into the clear water of the bowl.

He whimpered like a beaten dog.

The captain snapped his fingers at the men behind him. "The syringe." The man with the tray appeared at his side. Castro took an alcohol swab off the tray, pulled up the colonel's sleeve, searched briefly for a usable vein and swabbed it. The hallucinating prisoner seemed not to notice. Captain Castro reached for the syringe and injected a clear yellow liquid into the man's arm.

The whimpering stopped. The colonel's body went limp.

Captain Castro looked at his watch. The antidote only took a minute to work.

Slowly Colonel D. fell back into the arms of the captain. He motioned for help. The other white-coated man came forward and they lifted the unconscious colonel to his narrow bed.

Colonel D. opened his eyes. Each eyeball flicked madly back and forth over the faces of the men who stood above him. He started to groan and pushed himself away as if he still saw the deadly ghouls of his imagination.

"No, Colonel. No, it's all right now." Luis Castro leaned over him and spoke in a soft, soothing voice. "They have all gone away. Everyone. You are safe with us now." Castro took the colonel's limp hand and squeezed it. "They are all gone now."

The colonel relaxed visibly. Trust returned to his eyes.

"As long as you are here with us, you will be safe from them," Castro said. He knew exactly what he was talking about. He knew the unseen host that had attacked the colonel. He knew because he had ordered the specific dosage of the drug that gave a specific effect. He had even written the scenario and planted the seeds of it through hypnotic suggestion. He had found the colonel's devils and set them free to wreak havoc upon the colonel's psyche. It had not been all that difficult.

Who was the colonel most afraid of? His own victims, of course. The evil that he himself had done.

"Would you like to stay with me?" Captain Castro asked the colonel.

"Yes! Yes, please let me stay with you," the ex-torture master pleaded.

"Of course you can, Colonel. But you must tell us many things that we want to know. You must answer all our questions."

"Yes!" the colonel replied quickly, like a child promising to be good.

The man from Havana squeezed his hand tightly. "Good, Colonel. Then let us talk for a few hours. Then I will take you away from this prison forever." He motioned the others from the cell and flicked the tape recorder on.

BARRABAS UNWOUND THE STRING on the briefing case and snapped the seal. He pulled out a sheaf of government documents. Inside, among the standard briefings and bios he expected, were detailed maps of the Cuban coastline and intelligence photographs of the Sangrino Prison. There was also a diagram of the prison's interior done by an inside source.

The Sangrino had been built as a fortress by the Spanish in the eighteenth century. Now it was used as a prison for special inmates. Its sheer stone walls rose high above the rock promontory of a small peninsula. The peninsula in turn jutted out from the coastline inside a small circular bay. The entrance to the bay was narrow, only about two hundred feet across. It was guarded on either side by high stone bluffs, where listening posts were located. The harbor entrance was probably mined and definitely had security sensors.

Access to the prison could be gained only through underwater drainage conduits that emptied into the bay. From there it was merely a matter of memorizing the basic layout of the fortress to find the way to Colonel D.'s cell.

"Hayes!" Barrabas called over his shoulder into the house. A moment later the black man joined him on the terrace.

"Colonel?" Hayes pulled up a chair.

"What kind of shape is the boat in?" Barrabas gestured to the cruiser on the water.

"Tip-top, Colonel. It was the one Nanos and Lopez and Beck bought on a whim a while back. Before Lopez got killed. It was overhauled when we started this training because they planned to sell it when we finish."

"How long will it take to get us to Cuba?"

Claude Hayes looked at the colonel without blinking. If he was surprised by his commander's question, he gave no indication of it.

"About three hours, I'd say."

Barrabas looked at his watch. It was getting on toward midnight. "And what time's sunrise?"

"At 5:20 A.M., Colonel."

Barrabas nodded silently and looked pensively out over the water. After a few minutes, Hayes spoke again.

"Can I ask why?"

"Colonel?" Nate Beck stepped outside. "I determined the code variation and decoded a couple of documents. You won't believe it."

"Does it have something to do with Cuba?" Hayes asked.

"How'd you know?" Nate was surprised.

"Because the colonel is always there a step ahead of the rest of us," said Hayes.

"What's the story, Nate?" Barrabas asked.

"This X Command, they've set up some kind of rescue mission to get a guy out of the Sangrino Prison. The mission was set up for tonight."

Barrabas handed the papers from the briefing box to Hayes. "Have a quick look at these. I think we can get in and out by sunrise, but I wouldn't mind a second opinion. If we don't get out by sunrise, we won't get out at all."

The sound of the front door slamming came from inside the house.

"Come and get it, men. Food's on."

The three mercs pushed themselves up from their chairs and walked inside. Nanos and O'Toole were unpiling stacks of white takeout boxes on the table and opening the lids. The smell of exotic food wafted into the room.

Nate moaned. "I didn't realize how hungry I was."

"Colonel, this is the greatest food in the world," said Nanos enthusiastically. "And you'll never guess what kind."

Barrabas looked over the steaming boxes. "Looks like kosher Thai-Peruvian."

Nanos looked momentarily disappointed. "Okay, so I've been living in a cave for the past twenty years."

"Naw, it's not that, Alex," said Billy Two. "It's just that for you, eating means having your face buried in some..."

"Starfoot!" Nanos clenched his fist. "Eat this!"

"What's the matter, Alex? References to your life as a woman's man getting to you?" O'Toole gibed.

"Uh-uh. It's just that I haven't been getting any women lately. I'll be real glad when we've done our scuba training."

"Men, you all have an opportunity tonight to put that training to good use." Barrabas's voice commanded sudden attention. The men looked up from their food.

"Eat!" Barrabas ordered them. "I'll fill you in in the meantime."

As he explained the mission, the mercs lost their appetites, one by one.

"I don't feel hungry anymore." Nanos threw down his plate amid the ruins of the takeout dinner.

"Colonel, I looked through those plans," said Hayes. "If the four of us go in with scuba equipment, and depending on how long it takes us to dismantle any mines across the harbor, we'll get in and out within a couple of hours. Which will give us just enough time to get the cruiser out of Cuban waters by sunrise."

Barrabas stood and paced slowly to the window.

"The point is, what are we trying to do?" he asked as if he was talking to himself. "If we get Colonel D. first and take him out of there alive, we can bargain him as a trade for Tony Lopez. But if they get there first, we'll probably run into them on the way out. And we can relieve them of Lopez then. But—" he paused for a moment to consider his words "—I'm wondering if the trap is a trap."

"What do you mean, Colonel?" O'Toole asked.

"If I'm right, then we're being set up for something, for instance, to eliminate Colonel D., or to get him out alive, or even to go after X Command. It doesn't matter. The point is, when you know there's a trap and you go into it, it's a way of going on the offensive and turning it in on the people who set it.''

"And instead, maybe that's exactly what the enemy wants us to do," said Billy Two.

"Yup. Maybe we're walking into it with our eyes still closed. That would explain Tony Lopez."

"Well, there's only one thing worse than walking straight into a trap," said Nanos.

"What's that, Alex?" Beck asked.

"Sitting here waiting for something to happen."

Liam O'Toole's loud voice boomed. "So let's go for it, boys!" He pounded the flat of his hand on the table.

Barrabas looked at his men and broke into a smile. "That's what I like to hear."

12

Just beyond Cuba's territorial waters, a strange black-hulled sailboat with a forty-five-foot beam bobbed rhythmically on the rolling surface of the Caribbean. Bright lights from the cabin windows spilled through inky blackness and glowed on the surface of the water. The light was accompanied by the raucous voices of men at cards.

The leader of X Command stood on the bridge. He looked through infrared binoculars in the direction of Florida. Then he glanced at his watch. It was almost 3:00 A.M. The stars had disappeared behind a cloud, making the sea darker, with only a couple of isolated glimmering lights on the distant coastline of Cuba. The wind was picking up. The weatherman's predictions were right. He heard footsteps on the deck. It was George Hampton climbing up to the bridge.

"They coming yet?" he asked.

"Soon, George. The shore relay called up almost three hours ago. So they should be here very soon. By the way, they set off one of your little booby traps on their way into the beach house."

"They did!" Hampton was suddenly excited.

"Yeah. The one on the bottom door. But it didn't get anyone."

"That's impossible."

"Our people found no blood, no brains, no nothing, George. Just a doorframe blown to smithereens."

Hampton shook his head in wonderment. "How'd they do that?"

"I don't know. Then they broke a window and a door upstairs and got in without setting off any other traps. Too bad. It would've been nice to cut down on numbers a bit before we take them on face-to-face."

"So what's the plan again, Major?"

Braun lit a cigarette and offered one to Hampton. "After the SOBs clear the harbor entrance we can sail into the bay with the engines off. Meanwhile, a couple of the boys will plant explosives on the hull of the boat when they anchor. We'll get to the prison just in time to take Colonel D. off their hands, then leave them for the Cubans to handle. It should be very unpleasant for them. And with Colonel D. safe in Florida we can get down to business."

"Yeah," Hampton gushed enthusiastically. The business Braun referred to was the death-squad business. And as far as X Command was concerned, business was going to boom in the U.S. of A.

"What about the two kids?" Hampton asked.

Braun looked at him. "You want them, George?" he asked.

Big George smiled.

"You can have them. Long as you leave them dead when you're finished."

"Oh, they'll be dead all right. There won't even be pieces to send home to momma."

"Whatever turns you on, George." Braun raised the binoculars again and peered over the water. Suddenly he spoke, his voice curt and tense. "It's them. They're here."

A peel of laughter burst out from the cabin.

"Get downstairs and shut them up," Braun ordered. "And put the tape on in five minutes. It'll take another ten for them to pass us."

"What a great camouflage idea," said Hampton on his way downstairs.

"Sometimes the best cover is to have no cover at all," Braun replied as he disappeared.

Below deck the main stateroom was filled with smoke. Kid laughed loud and hard at the joke someone had just made. He leaned back from the table on the back legs of his chair, placed his hand of cards face-down and dragged hard on the thin cigar someone had given him. Around the table Zetmer and four other guys who were a part of X Command chuckled. Zetmer flicked his eyes at the Kid and back at his cards. He'd been looking at Kid like that all evening and the Kid couldn't figure out why. He just kept looking back with a big friendly smile. Zetmer never smiled.

"Hey, Tony!" Kid called across the room to Lopez who sat on a cushioned bench under the window. "Get over here and take a hand. Come on, lose your shirt." His voice was too loud and his words slurred slightly from the beer he'd been drinking.

Tony was falling asleep. He shook his head to clear it when he heard his name called and looked around, slowly comprehending what the Kid was saying. He shook his head again.

Kid lurched forward in his chair. "Come on!" he yelled.

"No, man." Tony shook his head again, more emphatically. "I don' wanna." He wasn't even sure he wanted to be there anymore.

By evening he had started to have doubts about the guys he was hanging around with and the realization sank in that Colonel Barrabas and the SOBs and his mother, were all going to be pissed with him. As for these guys, they might be mercs, and they sure had enough guns to prove it, but after a few hours Tony knew he didn't really like any of them. Not even the new ones who came along. Even Kid was kind of weird. But there wasn't much he could do about it, stranded on a boat out in the middle of the Caribbean on some mission they wouldn't even brief him on.

Right now, Tony just wanted to sleep.

But Kid wasn't taking no for an answer.

He stood up abruptly and walked toward Tony. He tried to swagger, but the roll of the boat and the alcohol in him turned it to a lurch. The other men stopped playing and watched.

Kid walked to the bench where Tony sat. "C'mon," he said defiantly.

"Uh-uh." Tony shook his head and looked up at the Kid towering over him.

"I said c'mon!" Kid's voice was getting mean. He grabbed Tony by the shoulder and tried to pull him. Tony shook his grip off. Kid grabbed him again.

"Man, I told you I don't wanna play. So hands off the fabric!" Tony grabbed the Kid's wrist and threw it back at him.

This time, Kid came back snarling. "An' I told you you'll play."

He reached down, grabbed Tony by the collar and hauled him up. He rammed him back against the wall.

"I don't want any trouble," Tony tried warning him.

He put his hands on top of Kid's to try to force them off his throat.

"Then play fucking cards!" Kid yelled, blowing spittle into Tony's face.

"Hey man, I don't need the shower." Tony wiped the spray from his face with the back of his hand in an exaggerated motion.

The men at the table laughed loudly at Kid.

"Fucking play cards!" he yelled again. He spun Tony around and sat him down hard in the empty chair. Then he grabbed the Uzi that had been lying nearby and shoved it hard against Tony's temple. His lips curled. "Now play cards," he said. He burst out in a shrill laughter. "Rat-a-tat-tat!" Tony stared deadpan at the table.

Kid leaned over to Tony's ear and spoke threateningly. "I just blew your fucking head off."

"Okay boys, cut the noise and get ready!" Big George's voice boomed from the cabin door. "They're coming. Bill, the major wants the tape on in five minutes. No more noise from now on."

The men broke up the card game and the table was folded against the wall. There was a flurry of activity as each man got ready.

Tony watched a moment before turning to Zetmer. "What should I do?" he asked.

Zetmer looked him in the face, cold and unfriendly. "Just stay put," he said, "till we're ready."

13

The passage to Cuba was smooth until the last hour, when the sky clouded over, obliterating the stars and leaving the sea in inky blackness. Soon the SOBs felt the wind pick up. When Barrabas suggested someone tune into a marine broadcast, they heard warnings of a gale approaching in a few hours from the east.

There was no sign of X Command, no sign of any other marine traffic save for a luxury schooner with an unusual black hull anchored just outside Cuban territorial waters. It was lit up like a Christmas tree from stern to bow, and the sounds of drunken merrymaking floated across the water, the braggadocio of men about to score and the shrill calls and giggling laughter of women who were resisting just to keep up appearances.

"Hmm, having a ball," Nanos mused from the bridge. "I could use some of that myself when we finish this." Barrabas peered at the boat with his binoculars. The stateroom curtains were closed and the bridge was deserted.

Nanos skillfully steered the cruiser silently past the luxury yacht and toward the dark line called Cuba a few miles ahead. The sounds and lights followed them over the water for a while before disappearing.

A thorough examination of the coastal maps of Cuba had shown them a sheltered cove less than a mile down the coast from the entrance to Sangrino Bay. Nanos, working off readings, guesstimates and coast-guard navigator's instincts, brought them to the exact spot. There the boat could sit in shallow water and be out of sight of passing coastal patrol boats.

Nanos turned off the engines while O'Toole dropped anchor from the bow. By the time the Greek joined the rest of the mercs on deck, Nate Beck, Claude Hayes and Barrabas were in wet suits and strapping the MKV1 scuba assembly on their backs.

"Move it, Alex," the colonel ordered. He zipped a waterproof case around an M-16 and handed it to Nanos. Hayes and Beck were almost ready to go, clipping knives and waterproof flashlights complete with inset compasses to their belts. In addition, the men distributed an assortment of explosives, some cable and chain cutters and a coil of rope among them. When each man was equipped, they sat on the edge of the deck and pulled on flippers.

O'Toole handed Barrabas a tightly bound bundle to slip on his back. It was an extra wet suit and tank for Colonel D.

"Can he swim?" O'Toole asked, tightening the straps.

"If he doesn't now," said Barrabas, "then he will by morning."

"It'll take us about ten minutes to get to the harbor entrance with these on," said Hayes, tightening one flipper. "After that, your guess is as good as mine. It depends on what we find going across the entrance."

Barrabas uncoiled the buddy line and threw it across the stern. Each merc grabbed a hook and snapped it onto his belt. In the black water it would keep them from getting separated and lost.

"Keep your eyes on the luminous compass on your flashlight," the colonel reminded them. "So if you do get separated and disoriented you can find your way back here." He took one last look at each of his men. "Ready?"

To a man, they nodded.

"Good luck, Colonel. And the rest of you," O'Toole said. "If Starfoot and I knew how to scuba we'd be out there with you."

"We need someone to run the boat, Liam," said Hayes.

"Yeah," Nanos added. "I have a feeling when we get back here we'll be in a big hurry to leave."

"With half the Cuban navy on our tail," Beck joked.

"Tail," said Nanos. "I'll keep reminding myself of what I have to look forward to when this is over with."

"Let's go!" Barrabas and Hayes pulled their face masks down and inserted their mouthpieces. Nate Beck and Alex Nanos followed suit. The four mercs simultaneously tipped into the water.

O'Toole and Billy Two watched the water bubble as the four bodies disappeared. Two waves covered the spot, and the surface of the sea appeared undisturbed. Then, one by one their lights came on, shining dimly under the surface and fading as they swam away.

"Now, we wait," O'Toole said softly, looking out over the dark cove and surveying the palm-tree-studded coastline. "And hope like hell Fidel Castro doesn't see us here."

Billy Two nodded silently and padded to the bow of the boat. As O'Toole watched him go, he noticed something funny about his walk. He looked. The Indian's feet were bare once again.

THE MILE-LONG UNDERWATER SWIM to the entrance of Sangrino Bay came off without any problems. They swam in a line, four abreast, with Claude Hayes slightly in the lead because of his experience. Claude steered. The others took note as they followed. The extra push power the flippers supplied thrust them quickly through the water. But in the total blackness under the surface, even the shallow swim quickly became claustrophobic. The water pressing against their wet suits seemed like the total darkness of night solidifying, as if it might thicken until it eventually crushed them.

It was something Barrabas had learned in the early days of his soldiering. Training is good to get past all the technical stuff and the tricks of the trade. But none of it combated the primordial instincts of the human animal: loneliness, boredom, fear. And on a murky, aqueous night ride like this one, the greedy yellow eyes of terror and panic leered at all of them through the impenetrable darkness of the water, daring them to lose control for even the briefest of moments. Once lost, gone.

Thirteen minutes after leaving the cruiser, Hayes came to an abrupt stop, twisting back to Barrabas and the other two mercs to draw them into a tight circle. He touched each man on the shoulder, tapping once, the signal to stop. He reached down and unhooked Nate Beck's buddy line, separating him from Barrabas and Nanos. Then he pointed his flashlight through the water.

Barely five feet ahead of them they saw the conical mine floating under the surface of the water.

They were in the harbor entrance.

Hayes motioned to Beck and then reached out to take him by the upper arm. He pulled him toward the mine. Then he turned back to face Barrabas and Nanos and pointed his flashlight again.

Another mine drifted at the end of its cable, a little farther off. Hayes swung the flashlight in a downward arc between the two mines to show them the cable that connected them in circuit. Hit one and they all went off. The cable was connected to ground monitors to alert surface troops that their underwater defenses were being tampered with.

Beck reached through the water and removed the coil of wire from his utility belt, handing the man his zip-cased M-16. Then Hayes and Beck swam into the darkness. Barrabas and Nanos waited.

A few minutes later, Hayes and Beck came to the rocky underwater wall that marked the cliffs enclosing the bay's entrance on one side. On the way they passed three more mines. There were probably seven or eight across the entrance altogether.

Hayes followed the cable with his light until they saw a connector embedded in a concrete fixture on the rock wall. Cables led upward to the surface and some kind of electrical source.

While Hayes held the light, Beck moved his hand over the connector, feeling its configurations. He found what he was looking for. A bolt. The bolt led to a female part, which was made for another cable and led to the same above-surface power source.

Beck reached into his belt and took out a pair of vise grips. A moment later, the bolt was free. He felt inside with his finger. The hole was filled with wax to protect the inside parts of the connector from saltwater damage. He took a small metal box from his belt with a two-inch-long male part extending from its bottom.

He inserted the male part into the female and pushed hard. The little metal plug pushed slowly through the hard wax. It was difficult to use enough force underwater, where the atmospheric pressure reduced a man's strength. Beck twisted the casing until he felt the plug hit hard against the bottom of the socket.

The little case contained a battery-powered circuit. Plugged into the connector, it would send out clear signals to ground sensors, which allowed them to disconnect the cable that the mines were strung on without alerting the surface monitors.

Just as he finished, he felt an eerie presence beside him. He looked. It was a large curious fish. Wanna watch, then watch, he said in the silence of his head. The fish turned and swam away.

Moving quickly, Beck withdrew the cable cutter from his belt and inserted the one-inch-diameter cable through the upper and lower jaws. He took the blasting cap that Hayes handed him and screwed it into the well at the top. Hayes had the hellbox.

The two men swam away from the cable a distance of twelve feet. The cutter was loaded with a quarter pound of Composition B—a mixture of TNT and cyclonite. It was guaranteed to blow the cable apart. There was also a very small chance that once the cable broke, the mines would go off one after another. They'd never know, if it happened.

Hayes pressed through the rubber pad in the hellbox and a tiny current flashed through the wires to the cable cutters.

They heard the strangely muffled hiss and sputter as the Composition B blew and the water frizzed up momentarily in turbulence. Then the loose end of the cable floated freely in front of them.

If they hadn't been sucking on oxygen, six feet under water, cheers would have whooped through the air.

They were too busy to celebrate, anyway. They grabbed the free end of the cable and began swimming it out to sea with powerful kicks. A few moments later they saw an underwater light flashing twice. It was Barrabas, answering in response to their light.

He and Nanos were waiting.

They grabbed the cable behind Nate Beck and Hayes and with four strong men on it, swung it quickly out to sea so that the necklace of mines now ran perpendicular to the shore.

Beck swam up beside the farthest mine in the chain with his vise grips out again. A moment later, he had the plug out of the mine's air compartment. It filled with water and sank quickly to the depths below, anchoring the mines in position.

The mercs snapped their buddy lines together and swam through the entrance of Sangrino Bay. Barrabas tugged three times on the buddy cord, telling his men to surface. In unison, they angled up and quietly broke the surface of the water between the two great cliffs that guarded the entrance.

Half a mile away the immense stone walls of the ancient Spanish fortress rose at the end of a rocky abutment that jutted into the bay.

Barrabas and the mercs treaded water with just their eyes above the surface and the occasional high wave lapping over their heads.

At each corner of the high prison walls there were round stone guard towers, and walkways ran along the ramparts between them. The stone walls were broken at the higher levels by thin slits, which had once been used by defenders of the fortress to protect themselves while they fired at the enemy outside. Now they were probably the windows of tiny cells.

A paved walkway ran a few feet above the water level around the base of the fortress. It was lit by lights set against the stone walls. On one side, Barrabas could make out something that hadn't been in Jessup's briefing papers. PT boats. At least two that he could see. Probably more.

And beside the guard towers on each corner klieg lights swept back and forth in slow arcs, splashing along the inner courtyard of the fortress and circling around to fall on the outer walls. The klieg lights were mostly for show, to let the inmates know they were being watched, night and day.

But the dark lines of equipment that were sometimes thrown into relief by the moving lights told Barrabas they had machine guns up there, too.

The four mercs disappeared under the water. Hayes led off once more, operating by compass alone, with the flashlight out. As they approached the base of the fortress, the lights occasionally splashed down through the water, casting eerie shadows over the blacksuited men. They swerved to avoid the light as much as possible.

Finally their progress was halted by the slime-covered stonework at the base of the fortress. Hayes steered them to the left, staying close to the wall and putting his hand out to feel along its surface. Twenty feet farther on they came to the end point.

A five-foot-wide circular passage was cut into the wall and covered with an iron grille. The bars were at least three inches in diameter, which spelled problems. Hayes had brought a bigger and more powerful cable and chain cutter, which could be used on an iron rod. But not that thick.

Momentarily nonplussed, the mercs silently tread water. Then Barrabas moved forward and ran his hand up and down one of the bars. He tugged. It didn't budge. But the metal was somewhat rusted. The bars hadn't been replaced in years. He tried the next one, moving his hand from top to bottom, feeling the decaying contours of the metal and prying away thick scales of rust. The other mercs saw what he was doing and quickly all four were testing each bar. Barrabas found the right one. It was near the center of the outlet. He peeled away enough scales of rust to take the bar down to less than two inches around.

He motioned to the others. Hayes was tamping a pound of plastic explosives into the jaws of the two-and-a-half-pound cable cutter. He handed it to Nate who attached the jaws to the top and bottom of the bar. Hayes motioned to Barrabas. The colonel couldn't make the signal out. Suddenly Hayes detached himself from the buddy line and swam off into darkness.

Barrabas screwed the priming adapter carefully into the activator well, then uncoiled the thin wires that led to the hellbox.

The mercs backed off.

Barrabas pushed the rubber pad over the detonator button.

Once more water hissed and bubbled furiously white as it boiled away from the explosion.

When it cleared, there was a two-foot-wide gap in the grate. Enough for a man to get through...without his airtanks. It was going to be tricky.

Barrabas went first. Keeping the mouth apparatus carefully in place and breathing slowly, he detached the MKV1 assembly and pulled it off his shoulders. Nanos held the tanks as Barrabas swam out of the vest. He took a breath, pulled the mouthpiece away and twisted it quickly back around the equipment before putting it back in his mouth. He could hear the mad stream of bubbles burst out and rise to the surface. Dangerous for detection, he thought.

With Nanos holding the scuba assembly and the mouthpiece securely in his mouth again, Barrabas turned himself around and backed legs first through the opening in the grate. When he was through, Nanos passed the tanks and assembly after him. Barrabas treaded with his back to the grate as Nanos strapped the assembly back on.

It was Nate Beck's turn next, and finally Alex's. Just as the three of them were inside, Claude Hayes reappeared. They helped him through. Barrabas noticed that two of the explosive packs that had been hanging from his belt were no longer there.

Underwater, he couldn't ask.

Barrabas glanced at the luminous dial of his diver's watch. It was almost 4:00 A.M. They were inside the Sangrino Prison. They had less than an hour to grab Colonel D. and get the hell out.

AFTER THE CRUISER CARRYING the SOBs had passed, Braun waited another ten minutes. The men of X Command, along with Kid and Tony, sat quietly in the stateroom. Some checked out their automatic rifles. Others looked off into space, listening to the high-pitched female giggles coming from the party tape Braun had on the reel-to-reel.

To any outside observers, the yacht was carrying a load of rich playboys and their stable of women. It was Braun's idea, and as a form of camouflage, he thought it was a pretty good one.

When enough time had passed, he snapped off the machine. The sudden silence made some of the men jump.

"Let's go!" Braun snapped loudly. The crew rushed for the cabin door. Braun turned to Kid and Tony who had also stood, waiting to be told what to do. "You two stay here."

"But..." Kid started to protest.

Braun pointed his finger. "Don't argue, either of you. It's insubordination. If you can't be disciplined, you'll have to be punished. That's the first thing you learn."

"Yes, sir!" Kid said, eager to please. Tony nodded slowly. He knew something was wrong here. He just couldn't figure out what it was.

"I'll come down and get you when we're ready." Braun turned and left the stateroom.

By the time he got to the deck his men had the black sails billowing in the strong northeasterly. The yacht gathered speed as it sailed across the surface of the water. The coastline of Cuba emerged as a thin line on the horizon, darker than the rest of the night. Braun watched it come closer from the bridge.

By the time they got within a half mile of the shore, the boat was moving at a fair clip. Zetmer was at the helm.

"There it is." Braun pointed ahead of them and slightly to the starboard side. Almost invisible against the dark coastline was a cleft in the rocks. The entrance to Sangrino Bay.

Zetmer turned the wheel slightly to alter course. The big mainsail ballooned, rippling across one corner.

"Keep our speed up, Bill," said Braun.

Zetmer nodded and spoke slowly and softly into the intercom box beside his head. Somewhere on the deck someone pulled in the mainsail.

Braun descended to the deck. His own two-man diving team was wet-suited and ready. They sat on the gunwale with their scuba assemblies in place. When they saw Braun they pulled their masks down. Braun flicked his eyes over both men. Each carried an explosive pack, a sheath knife, a flashlight and a pistol in a waterproof carrying case. One had a small attachment to his utility belt that emitted a low-frequency radio signal.

"Ready to go?" Braun asked them.

They both nodded. One leaned over and pulled a conical metal buoy from the deck. It was attached to a long rope and the rope was attached to a heavy anchor.

"It goes over when we do," one of them said.

"I'll run through it again," Braun told them. "The cove where they're anchored is about a mile east of here. After you're finished, you come back the same way you went in. Follow your compass bearings exactly. When you're close, you can switch the remote radio signal on and the buoy will light up. Not brightly and not for very long. You wait by the buoy. We'll grab you as we go by on our way out. And I warn you, we'll be going fast. Don't miss our lines. We aren't turning back."

The two divers nodded.

Braun gave them the signal to go.

They put their mouthpieces in. One held the anchor and the other the buoy. Simultaneously, both men went over the edge into the jet waters.

Braun turned around and called to Hampton, who was standing by the steps to the bridge. "Get the rest of the men into their wet suits," he said. Hampton scurried off.

X Command's boat sailed straight for the rocky cleft that led into Sangrino Bay.

14

Once again Claude Hayes led the way through the narrow underwater conduit, with Barrabas, Beck and Nanos following the glow of his light. The water was ice-cold, numbing their faces and bare hands. It seemed impossible that anything could be darker under the surface of the ocean on a starless, moonless night. This was. It was also much longer than indicated on the plans he had studied. He had expected a twenty-foot swim. They had already gone fifty or sixty.

Finally Hayes stopped the others and jerked the buddy line three times. Surface. The mercs had hit the end of the line.

They began swimming straight up in a vertical stone well. Twenty feet later, they broke the surface of the water.

The beam from Hayes's flashlight danced along the stone walls. On one side, a waterfall poured down from high above. The men could hear a rustling noise on stone ledges above their heads.

"Rats," Barrabas whispered, pulling the mouth apparatus away and breathing the air. It was foul and rank, the smell of sewers.

"Shit," cursed Nanos. "I hate rats."

"Over here," they heard Hayes calling to them. He was shining light on the iron rungs of a ladder set into the stone wall. Barrabas already had his flippers off and hooked to his belt. He grabbed the first rung and pulled himself up.

He knew he was at the top when the air suddenly became fresher and wafted against his wet skin. He put his hand over the top of the wall and felt the stone floor. A moment later he was sitting on it. He took his flashlight from his belt and turned it on.

He was standing in a small tunnel of stone, with a walkway about five feet wide on one side. The rest of it was water. A stream of it, cold and dark, flowing quickly from high up in the fortress. Probably it was a combination of sewage, rainwater and an underground stream.

Hayes clambered up the ladder next, followed by Beck and Nanos. The mercs quickly stripped off their MKV1 scuba gear and unzipped the cases of the M-16s. The cold steel clicks of magazines injected echoed in the stone chambers. They were going to leave the scuba tanks there, along with the extra for Colonel D., until they came back for the return trip.

Barrabas waited until they were all ready, then he turned and led them quickly along the walkway, farther into the underground recesses of the ancient Spanish fortress.

The tunnel was low, a little too low for a man more than six feet tall. Barrabas and Hayes both had to walk with their heads slightly bowed. Their flashlights glistened off the slime-covered stone walls. Water dripped from between the crevices in the ceiling. One drop came down with enough accuracy to fall inside the collar of Barrabas's wet suit. It felt like death touching its fingers to the back of his neck.

The sound of running water grew louder as they progressed. Once again, it was farther than the diagrams indicated. Finally the noise of the water was almost deafening. Barrabas saw the end of the tunnel.

A waterfall poured through a narrow opening in the stone about four feet above the bottom of the tunnel. On one side, at the end of the walkway, rungs set in the stonework led up to a small iron door.

Barrabas slung his M-16 over his shoulder and mounted quickly. He grabbed the rusty handle of the door. It didn't budge. There was no time to fool around and try to persuade it.

"Hayes," he hissed down into the darkness. "A half pound of explosives."

A hand reached up to give him a block of soft plastique. He tamped it into the crevices near the hinges and on the other side where the handle was, feeling his way in the darkness.

He reached down again. Hayes's hand was there again, this time with the detonator wires. He inserted them into the plastics and quickly descended.

Hayes gave him the hellbox. The mercs retreated back down the tunnel as far as the wires let them and pressed themselves tightly against the cold wet walls. They covered their ears and averted their faces from the direction of the door.

Barrabas pressed the button.

The explosive boomed and the boom echoed up and down the narrow tunnel, pounding into the stonework. Bits of moldering masonry fell from the ceiling near the falls, splashing into the cold running water.

The iron door fell back through the disappearing smoke. It bounced heavily on the stone wall and clanged on the top rung of the ladder before clattering down into the tunnel.

"Shit, Colonel. You figure they heard that?" Nanos asked, breathing heavily in relief.

"Nope."

"You sure?"

"Uh-huh. 'Cause if they did, we're in big trouble. Let's go."

Barrabas hopped over the now-detached door and climbed quickly back up the iron rungs where he pulled himself into the dark hole where the door once was. The others soon followed.

The stone corridor they were in was dry compared to where they'd just been. The mercs could hear the low distant hum and throb of machinery. They were higher in the fortress and near the utility plant. From forty feet or so farther on, where the corridor ended in a T, came the faint glimmer of an electric light.

Barrabas led the way. At the T he stopped, remembering from the plans he had studied that the left way ended in the electrical and water utility plant, and the cell blocks were to the right. He turned back and spoke to Nate Beck.

"I want you to stay here. Hayes!" He called to the black man. "Give him some plastics." Then he pointed to the stone ceiling. "Line a few of the blocks up there with explosives and bring the wires down. If we're lucky we won't have to use it. But we might be coming back in a real hurry and need something to distract whoever's coming after us. Otherwise, just stay out of sight and wait. If it takes us longer than twenty minutes, it'll take us forever."

In their line of work, forever meant never again.

Barrabas took the rest of the corridor in a loping half run, landing silently on the pads of his soft leather boots. The corridor twisted with a sharp left turn and again to the right. Every twenty feet another very dim, low-watt bulb in a metal cage weakly illuminated the way. Now the plans were accurate. At the end of the final stretch another metal door stood open. On the other side, stone steps went upward.

Barrabas and his men didn't stop.

They took the steps three at a time in long even jumps until they came to the top. Another door led to a corridor. A long corridor. A left turn led eventually to a major security area. Colonel D.'s cell was on the right.

The mercs paused before the last push to catch their breath. Holding the folding-stock M-16 like a handgun, Barrabas leaned against the left side of the doorframe and slowly moved his head so that one eye peered into the corridor. One way was clear. The other way wasn't. About forty feet down, just past a couple of small steps, a guard stood watch.

He paced slowly in a crisp uniform and wore a steel helmet. Guarding a prisoner deep in the bowels of an old stone fortress wasn't hard work, but it was boring, and the boredom showed in the young guard's face. Barrabas pulled his head back.

He raised his hand and showed one finger to Hayes and Nanos.

He pulled a metal clip from his belt and with a low underhand, bounced it into the corridor. The clip pinged twice before coming to a stop against the far wall.

Barrabas listened.

First he heard the sound he wanted. Footsteps approaching. He signaled to Hayes and Nanos. They pressed against the door, out of sight.

The slow footsteps became louder. They stopped, shuffled quietly, climbed two stone steps and stopped again. The guard was looking for the source of the noise. Then the footsteps continued.

Far enough for Barrabas to see him just outside the door. He was turning around, looking to the left and right.

Too late.

As noiselessly as a shadow, as fast as the breeze, Barrabas was behind the man pulling him backward and off-balance. Before the soldier could react, Barrabas had his helmet pulled off. He bashed the rounded top into the back of the guard's head just above his neck. The man slumped, unconscious, falling back into Barrabas's arms. The mercenary leader pulled the limp body into the stairwell.

"Tie him up!" he hissed, moving back to the door to look out again. It was a very lucky break for the soldier that he had been sloppy enough not to snap his helmet strap in place. Otherwise his neck would have broken over Barrabas's forearm.

Nanos and Hayes left the soldier bound and gagged and still unconscious, tucking the body well behind the door. Barrabas looked at them. They nodded. They were ready.

He glanced into the corridor. Still clear. They went for it.

The four soldiers ran down the corridor, leaped over several short steps and past rows of doors that led to tiny cells. They headed for the one on the right side at the end. Even before they got there Barrabas knew they were in trouble.

The door to Colonel D.'s cell stood ajar.

MEANWHILE, ON THE CRUISER, Billy Two and Liam O'Toole paced silently and waited for their fellow fighters to return. They did not speak.

Occasionally O'Toole watched Billy Two standing bare chested at the edge of the boat. The light sea breeze blew his long black hair back and fluttered the feathers that were woven into it. The painted lines on his face and arms glowed slightly in the dark.

O'Toole shook his head sadly. There had been a time, once, when Billy Two was as boisterous as the rest of them, engaging in that lively cheeky banter that was a natural part of a mission involving fighting men. But not now. Not since Spetsnaz and the Russian psychiatric institute had finished with him.

Billy Two had been left alive, but badly damaged. If O'Toole had been in Barrabas's place, he wouldn't have let Billy Two come, even for the ride. A bow and arrows. A fucking bow and arrows, he brings with him. The guy was nuts. O'Toole shook his head sadly.

At the stern of the boat, Billy Two wasn't feeling sad at all.

He was listening.

To the hushing sound of the wind in the palm trees that lined the shore, to the soft gurgle of water lapping against the sides of the boat.

And something else.

Something he wasn't sure of.

Something in the water that shouldn't be there.

He listened hard, trying to filter out the steady sounds of wind and sea, trying to hook into the almost imperceptible difference he sensed.

He walked closer to the stern of the boat, cocking his head to the side. There it was. The sloshing sound of a single wave was somehow disturbed, thrown out of the smooth rhythm of the other waves.

An animal sound.

The human animal.

The man-beast.

Billy Two opened his eyes wide to let the night flood in, casting them like nets over the black water.

He sniffed the air.

Somehow he knew there were two of them and he knew exactly where they were.

He put his hand on the knife in the sheath at his side, just to feel it there.

O'Toole watched him step high up onto the gunwale. He was about to call out for him to stop, but Billy Two was gone. Liam rushed to the stern of the boat.

Billy Two's long body cut through the water like a blade, his outstretched hands opened with just the tips of his thumbs together. In the seconds it took for his dive to slow, he encountered that which he sought. The neck of a man-beast. The Indian's hands closed like the grips of a steel vise. His thumbs began a relentless inward pressure. Flesh yielded. The two bodies surfaced. Billy Two saw the eyes of his victim through his mask. The eyes were red like the devil's and black with death. His fingers and thumbs pressed harder. The diver's mouth apparatus fell limply from the man's mouth, followed by drool, the sounds of a larynx crunching and the full extent of tongue beginning to swell.

A voice whispered into Billy Two's ear. "Behind you, Starfoot."

He was thankful for the noise. He could feel the water

behind and underneath swirl with the turbulence of a swimmer coming up from the depths, and he knew it was another beast.

This one's friend.

His enemy.

He took a deep breath, filling his lungs to capacity until they ached, swelling against his diaphragm and rib cage.

He pushed down with his outstretched arms, pulling the diver's head underwater, the last light of life in the man's eyes snuffed out by the waves as his head disappeared beneath the surface. Billy Two kicked his legs forward, spread them wide and snared them around his opponent's chest and waist, pinning his arms to his sides. He squeezed his legs and crossed his ankles. The steel pincers locked him in place, holding the man in the depths.

Billy Two was a merman now. He let go of the man's neck and arched his body with his head bent, his chin almost touching his chest. He pulled himself forward and down with a powerful breaststroke. The man trapped between his legs was drag, but Billy's body descended, and he saw his second opponent coming up to meet him. He saw the white blade of a knife. The Indian reached for his.

Too late!

He felt the sting of steel sharp against him as the blade stroked across his back and side, barely missing his kidney.

Blood gushed and mixed with wild water.

Billy Two opened his legs, leaving the first beast to thrash his way to the surface. The drag was gone. He'd take care of it in a minute. He bent his neck down again and pulled himself farther down into the water.

His heart pounded like a freight train and the oxygen strained to escape his lungs.

Not yet, he thought.

His heart eased off.

He was under the second diver now, but the enemy was turning. Billy did a reverse stroke to stop his descent and brought himself to a vertical position. He scissors-kicked his muscular thighs and calves once. It drove him upward like a missile from its silo, his arms extended over his head, his knife of cold sharp steel, deadly steel, aimed straight up.

Point of impact.

The loser's belly.

The knife cut through rubber wet suit into soft gut mass.

Billy Two kicked again, driving his body higher until he came up beside the diver, and with his left arm he reached around his body. His broad outstretched hand clamped to the man's chest. He kicked again, driving both of them upward. *Air* was the word he heard in his brain, the one and only word.

All else was automatic: fist clenched to the handle of the knife; knife twisted and turned to slash and cut; pulled from man's stomach loosing blood and gut matter; knife plunged hard into man's chest; man's body stiffening as blade pierced heart; man dying.

Gripping the diver with his left arm and with his right fist around the knife and flush to the man's chest, Billy Two's head and shoulder cleared the water like the sudden surfacing of a submarine. He thought he heard someone calling. He sucked air.

He pulled the knife from the chest of the dead diver and let the body go. It sank beneath the waves. He heard splashing and thrashing. It was the first opponent, still alive and trying to swim for shore.

With five powerful strokes in a heads-up crawl, Billy Two was on him. He came up behind the man and forked his elbow around his neck. With his right he felt down the man's body. He found a knife. The knife came out of the sheath and was dropped. It sank to the endless nothing of the sea bottom.

The man was crying and whimpering with fear. Billy Two cupped his left hand around the man's chin, and with a reverse scissors kick, right hand outstretched and stroking gently, he began the swim back to the boat.

O'Toole was waiting for him at the stern. "Shit, Billy. Here, let me give you a hand. What the hell was going on out there? Shit."

Liam O'Toole rarely got upset. This was one of those rare times.

"Take this," said Billy, swinging the weak man around. "Under the armpits." With powerful kicks he was able to hold the man high in the water. O'Toole reached down, hooked his hands under the man's shoulders, and they hoisted the diver over the side of the boat. He flopped onto the deck like a fish out of water. O'Toole began stripping the mask and tanks off as Billy Two came up the ladder.

"Why didn't you come in to help?" Billy asked O'Toole, shaking water from his hair and eyes.

O'Toole looked up at him apologetically. "Shit, Billy. I can't swim."

"Can't swim?"

O'Toole nodded. His eyes spoke of great shame. Billy Two shrugged. "We all have our talents," he said.

The diver suddenly began to struggle as O'Toole pulled down the zipper of his wet suit. His eyes were wide with fear and he tried to scramble away from the two men.

Billy Two took one long step forward and grabbed the man by the wet suit. He had big, ugly bruises around his throat. He yelped, remembering the hands that made the bruises.

"Tell us what we must know," Billy commanded. "Everything."

The man spoke hoarsely, a few words at a time, sucking air back through his slightly crushed trachea. His eyes flickered in a wild dance. He looked at death.

"X Command. Major Braun sent us. To plant explosives on your boat. We followed you from Florida."

"Where is X Command?" Billy's fist clenched harder and more persuasively.

"At the Sangrino Prison. Your man, Barrabas, and the others cleared the mines. X Command sailed through. It's a trap."

Billy Two had heard enough.

He twisted himself around behind the man's back and crossed both arms around his neck. He jerked once with incredible rage. There was a grinding crunch. The man went limp. Death froze his eyes.

Billy dropped the body, the head bent back at an impossible angle. He picked up the corpse and hurled it into the water.

"You're bleeding, Billy." O'Toole pointed to the long stream of blood clotting along the wet skin of his lower back and staining his water-soaked pants.

"It's nothing. We must go to Barrabas."

O'Toole nodded. "I can drive. You fix that up." Billy Two reached with both hands into his long stringy hair and started disentangling the now bedraggled feathers.

"Now, Starfoot! That's an order. First the wound. Then the feathers."

Billy smiled. The white man with the red hair was a great warrior, even if he couldn't swim. But the white man would never understand.

"You drive," said Billy Two. "I will fix the wound."

15

Barrabas, Hayes and Nanos fanned out around the open door of the cell with their guns poised and ready to fire right into the surprised faces of Luis Castro and the infamous Colonel D.

"I see we are too late," the Cuban officer said solemnly, eyeing the three American mercs.

Barrabas moved in, his eyes flicking quickly around the cell while he held his M-16 up with both hands. He was raw, running on nerves, his whole body on battle alert. Nanos followed him into the cell. Hayes stayed in the corridor.

"Up against the wall, Cuban," he ordered Castro.

The man walked slowly to the far wall. Barrabas thought he noticed a slight smile on his face. It puzzled him. He saw the tape recorder on the table.

"So, you have come to liberate the greatest torturer the Americans have ever seen," the Cuban said. "This is what your great democracy means. The freedom to brutalize people."

"Shut up," Barrabas ordered. "You." He pointed at Colonel D. "We're taking you out of here. Nanos—tie up the Cuban."

Nanos went toward Castro. The Cuban kept talking.

"Another few minutes and I would have had our notorious Torture Master safely on his way to Havana.

There, he would have rotted away in another prison. The world would have been much safer without him free in it. But you Americans..."

The Cuban was forced down onto the floor as Nanos tied his legs.

"You cannot leave well enough alone. Now you will take this evil man to America and set him free. But his freedom will be our victory. All the oppressed people of the world will see what your country stands for."

"Not free," Barrabas growled.

Luis Castro smiled mockingly. "Not free! Then why are you here? To take him to America to face trial?"

"Something like that," Barrabas said. "Okay, let's lift him belly down onto the bed. Tie his ankles to his hands."

"And gag him," Nanos added, removing a strip of tape from a pocket on his web belt.

Luis studied the white-haired warrior. "I will remember you," he said. His voice was cut off as Nanos slapped the adhesive tape over his mouth.

"Ain't that life," the Greek said. "Every day we seem to make another enemy."

In a moment they were finished. Barrabas pushed the speechless and frightened Colonel D. out of the cell and motioned for Nanos to follow. Barrabas turned to take one last look at Luis Castro, bound and gagged on the prison bed. "The name's Barrabas. He won't go free. Not if I have anything to do with it. It's not what we came for." They started to retrace steps through the prison.

The Cuban gazed at the colonel steadily. It was all he could do. Barrabas left.

The mercs raced back through the corridors, past the

still-unconscious soldier by the door, down the stone steps and into the lower corridor.

Colonel D. was fearful and hesitant. Finally Nanos grabbed his upper arm and pulled him along to keep his speed up. He had not yet spoken a word, not even of protest or a demand for an explanation. There was something wrong with him. Barrabas caught the needle marks on his arms as they rushed along.

Finally they came to the left turn off the T where they had left Nate Beck. But Beck was nowhere to be seen. The mercs quickly checked out the stonework and saw the plastic explosives tamped into place in the low stone ceiling. Detonator wires led down the crevices. But no Nate.

"Keep going," Barrabas told them.

Hayes led and Barrabas went last. They held their M-16s in their right hands and flicked their flashlights on as they moved into the darkness of the final passage-way. They reached the hole that led down into the drainage conduit. Hayes went first, turning and lowering himself on the iron ladder. Finally Colonel D. began to react. He wimpered with fear.

"Come on," Nanos growled.

"You go," Barrabas snapped. "I'll hand him to you."

Nanos backed through the opening. Barrabas lifted the colonel by his collar and the back of his pants, lowering his legs to Nanos. The death master whined incoherently and clawed at Barrabas's shirt. The merc leader reached back and gave him a hard backhand across the face. Colonel D.'s eyes rolled, but he stopped whining.

Once the prisoner was through, Barrabas followed. At the bottom he turned to his two soldiers, their faces ghostly, lit by Hayes's flash.

"Beck here?"

The two men shook their heads.

"Shit!"

Then they heard the worst of all possible things. A metal sound. The sound of a bolt sliding back on a rifle.

A single brilliant beam almost blinded them. Three men stepped forward, one a little ahead of the other two. The fourth held the light.

They all held guns.

"Drop them if you want to see your buddy alive again," the man in front said.

Barrabas paused, thinking fast and wild. But all his thoughts ended in a round of death for the house.

He slowly dropped his rifle.

Hayes and Nanos waited longer.

"Drop them," he told his soldiers.

They could hear moans coming from behind the brilliant light.

"That's your buddy. Yes, he's alive. So far."

Barrabas recognized the voice. The trap had been sprung. It was Major Braun.

"So, Barrabas. We meet again. Small world, isn't it?"

"Too small when it comes to scum like you, Braun," Barrabas replied. Lit from behind, the man's face was a hollow pit of darkness.

"Scum like me?" Braun said incredulously. "It surprises me to hear you say it. I'm the one, after all, who believes in what I'm doing. I have a cause to fight for. And I believe in it."

"And what's that?"

"To get rid of the filth and the scum who are out to destroy America. The Commies and the fags."

"And the niggers. And the Jews," Hayes added softly, his voice brittle with anger and contempt. "I know your kind, the kind that believe in causes."

"Shut your man up, Barrabas. Or I will. Permanently."

Barrabas didn't move.

"You disgust me," Braun continued. "You come across like a guy out to save the world, but let's face it. You do it for the money. Like in Rhodesia, Angola, Bolivia. For anyone who pays. And because you're a killer."

"That's right, Braun. I'm a mercenary. I don't believe in causes. I've seen enough causes come and go, and on their way out they drag the corpses of their victims with them. Sure, I'm a professional. I pick and choose what suits me. On my terms. But I don't try to make it sound any better than what it really is."

"How noble," Braun said sarcastically. "We'll take Colonel D. off your hands now. He has some important work to do for us in America. Zetmer, take care of your old teacher."

Zetmer and another commander stepped forward and went to the frightened colonel, pulling him to their side of the walkway.

While they moved, Braun talked.

"Our plan worked like a charm, Barrabas. We needed Colonel, D. Other interested parties wanted you out of the way. We pooled resources. You went off in pursuit of Colonel D., opening the way for us to come in after you. You the hunter were in fact being hunted."

"The yacht we passed..."

"That's right. That was us. The partiers, the merrymaking you heard was all a tape recording. A clever little bit of camouflage.''

"And Tony Lopez."

"Stumbled into it. When first you refused to take the mission because of Lopez, we were...concerned. Worried that our plans might fail. But we were able, through some good fortune of our own, to turn the boy's stupidity to our own advantage.''

"Where is he now?"

"Safe. With us. For the time being. In a moment we're going to leave. If any of you try to stop us, Tony Lopez will die. Slowly.''

Barrabas didn't doubt Braun's threat.

"We're ready," Zetmer told his leader. The X Commandos had pulled a wet suit on Colonel D. and had strapped the scuba apparatus on his back.

"Good," Braun said. Then he smiled at Barrabas. "Show these mercenaries their fellow soldier.''

The man holding the light turned it against the wall.

Nate Beck was spread-eagled, his arms pinned by knives piercing his biceps. His agony was obvious.

"No!" Nanos shouted and rushed to help his comrade.

An X Commando stepped forward and bashed the butt of his rifle into Nanos's stomach. The Greek doubled over in his own agony. A fist smacked into his face. Then a second fist. The Greek crumpled and fell semiconscious to the floor.

"Now show them their equipment," Braun ordered. The light moved down. On the stone floor, the SOBs' air tanks and scuba assemblies lay in pieces. The valves on the tanks had been opened, the air bags and hoses slashed.

"Get their flashlights." One of his men did as he was instructed. Braun threw them into the water.

"Take their guns?" one of the men asked.

"No. Leave them their guns. They will have to fight the Cubans on their way out. I know Barrabas's fighting spirit. He will take lots of Cubans with him. But, ultimately, they will be overpowered. If they do not die from Cuban bullets, they will die from Cuban torture."

Braun stepped back. "Go!" he ordered his men. Two of them slipped into the murky water, holding a whimpering and semihysterical Colonel D. between them.

"Give me the light!" The fourth man handed Braun the high beam. The X Command leader smashed it against the stone wall, plunging the tunnel into pitch-blackness.

The mercs heard the splash of bodies hitting the water, then the sound of the water dripping from stones, and the silence of total darkness.

INSIDE SANGRINO BAY, a few hundred yards offshore and taking its cover from the night, the black-sailed yacht awaited the return of Major Braun.

One man stood watch on deck. He glanced at his watch as the second hand ticked away the minutes. Braun and the others would return soon with Colonel D. in tow. The sooner the better. The klieg lights, flashing along the walls of the fortress and the walkway below, made the guard very nervous. The wind was picking up and he felt the first drops of rain.

Below deck, in the stateroom, a more gleeful drama unfolded.

George Hampton was getting his kicks at Tony Lopez's expense.

"Hey, Tony. We got something for you to do now."

"Oh, yeah?" Tony answered suspiciously.

"Yeah. Here. Put this pack on." Hampton handed him a small rucksack. "C'mon, quick."

"What's in it?"

"I'll explain as I strap it on. Come on. We don't have much time."

A little reluctantly, Tony swung the rucksack around his shoulders, pulling the straps over his arms. Hampton quickly tightened the straps.

"Hey, not so tight," Tony protested, squirming to loosen it.

"Yeah, sure, it's got to be tight." Hampton's hands moved quickly and he spoke breathless with excitement.

"Yeah? What's in it?"

"Two and a half pounds of TNT."

Silence. Tony pondered the words. "No," he said in disbelief.

"Yeah," George affirmed enthusiastically.

Kid, who had been watching with interest, broke out into a peal of ridiculing laughter. Just as Tony started to struggle, Big George grabbed his arms, forcing them behind his back and locking his wrists together. Tony kneed him in the groin.

Hampton bent over in pain. "You little..." He struck out with his fist, slamming Tony in the eye. The teenager fell back, thrown off-balance by the rucksack. Kid flew across the room and grabbed Tony's legs. Tony fell forward onto the floor. He kicked and yelled and tried to pry himself out of Kid's clutches and make for the door.

Kid laughed uncontrollably as he gripped Tony's legs. Hampton moved menacingly toward Tony and grabbed the struggling boy's arms. He held them with one hand, pressing his knee into the small of Tony's back. In the other hand he had rope. He started tying. When he finished with the hands he gagged Tony and started on the feet.

Kid stood back and mocked the teenage boy. "Ha ha, sucked you in real good Tony. Real good."

"Yeah," George joined in with a little chuckle. "You were the bait, Tony. To lure the SOBs here. Didn't you know? Those terrorists we were after, they're really just your old buddies Colonel Barrabas and the SOBs. You helped us get them. How's it feel to betray your old buddies, Tony?" He laughed.

Tony suddenly stopped struggling and squirming when he heard the word "betray." The reality of what was really happening sunk in, a weight heavier than the knee pressing in on his back, and far more painful.

"Look at him, he's crying." Kid pointed and laughed. Tears clouded Tony's eyes and scalded his cheeks. Oh shit, he thought. Like a baby. He hadn't cried ever before that he could remember.

George finished tying him up. He went to a duffel bag nearby and withdrew a long coil of rope. Tony could feel him opening the rucksack and fiddling around.

"What is it?" the Kid asked.

"Wire-bound primacord," Hampton explained, attaching it to the TNT inside the rucksack.

"Primacord? What's that for?"

George gave the Kid a sideways glance. His eyes said things but the Kid wasn't listening.

"It's a waterproof cord with a petrin core. Petrin is a very sensitive explosive. When I attach a blasting cap to the end of the cord, and when I detonate the blasting cap, it'll explode at a rate of 21,000 feet a second. Very, very fast. Instantaneously, you could say. And Tony Lopez will go boom.''

"Ha ha ha. Hear that, Tony? Sucked you in real good." Kid looked at George again. "Where?"

"I'll throw him overboard," said George, finishing the connection inside the rucksack and snapping it shut. "I'll coil out the primacord, attach it to a thousand feet of detonator wire. Then, as we sail out of the harbor, there'll be a big bang to surprise the Cubans. And no more Tony Lopez. Just McNuggets for the fishies."

"What a great idea, George. Great idea. I'll help you throw him over."

"No, you won't," George said, standing up.

"Sure. Why not?"

"Because I can attach as many little bundles of explosives to the primacord as I want. At least two." He walked toward the Kid.

"Oh yeah?"

"Yeah. And guess what?"

"What?" Kid stopped laughing. He saw the look in George's eyes. He didn't want to believe it.

"You're the second bundle." He reached out his hands for the Kid.

"Heh heh. That's a good joke, George."

"No joke, Kid."

"But what do you mean? I've been helping you out." Kid backed away from the approaching man.

"Yeah. You been a great help, Kid. But we don't need any more help from you." George grabbed him. Kid struggled and protested.

"Major Braun doesn't know about this. No! Stop! He doesn't know. He'll be mad if you..." George lifted the Kid by the shoulders and slammed him back against the wall. Kid's eyes went wide with total terror.

"You can't, you can't do this," he yelled.

"So who's gonna stop me?" said George evenly. He grabbed the Kid, threw him onto the floor and went down with the knee in the back. Kid tried to squirm away, yelling and pleading. George calmly grabbed both his wrists and forced his arms down. "Who's gonna stop me?" he said, this time to no one in particular.

16

The wind picked up. As Liam O'Toole steered the boat between the cliffs that led into the bay, the first big fat raindrops began to splatter down onto the deck.

He cursed as breakers rolled high under the boat, and he gripped the wheel harder. He wasn't particularly experienced at anything to do with boats or water. He was a soldier, an ex-army sergeant with expert training in sabotage and demolitions. Firmly land based. All this wet stuff was a little out of his league.

Down on the bow, looking steadily across the dark waters of the bay at the old fortress, Billy Two stood erect, his face lifted up to the rain. His chest was bare. At least O'Toole had persuaded him to tie a bandage at his waist just above his blood-drenched pants.

Suddenly the Osage warrior loped back to the stern and climbed to the bridge.

"There is a boat. There." He pointed to the port side.

"Where?" O'Toole blinked, trying to pry the darkness apart with his eyes. Then he made it out. It was big and black, with a billowing black sail rising up the mast. "It's the one we passed on the way in here." He grabbed the binoculars and looked again, simultaneously steering the cruiser in that direction.

It was difficult in the rolling seas, the rain and darkness, but as they came closer he could make out movements at the stern of the mysterious ship. Men were climbing from the water into the boat. O'Toole's hand on the throttle tightened and pushed forward. It wouldn't move. It was already on full speed. The cruiser plowed rapidly across the bay, nearing the black sailboat, smashing its way against high, rolling storm waves. The rain had begun to pelt now, and in the distance thunder boomed. O'Toole muttered another Irish curse. Lightning would be serious trouble if it illuminated the boats on the bay for the guardians of the machine guns in the fortress half a mile away.

"The thunder will hide us," Billy Two said into his ear. "The sound of our engines."

O'Toole nodded. That was the other side of it. But now the resistance from the high water was pulling the steering wheel in the wrong direction. He gripped hard and swung back. "But not the sound of gunfire!" he yelled back at Billy Two over the sound of the rain.

The Indian didn't answer. He jumped down onto the lower deck and disappeared into the cabin. O'Toole muttered to himself as he jerked the wheel into line. "Stuck out on high seas in the middle of a tropical storm in shooting distance of two different enemies with only a loony Indian for a friend."

He heard the slap of Billy's feet running up the steps again. The black sailboat was only a couple of hundred feet away now. He saw blacksuited shadows skulk on the deck. They threw something overboard. Then something else. It looked like bodies. "Oh, Christ, no," Liam O'Toole muttered. "Please, sweet Mary, say it ain't so."

And if the thought that Barrabas and the SOBs had finally bought it wasn't enough, Liam O'Toole sudden-

ly saw a sight on the cruiser's bow that almost made him
want to jump overboard and swim to Florida. Illuminated in the first bright flash of lightning, bare-chested
and defiant, stood Billy Two.

With the goddamn bow and arrow.

He saw the warrior speak and through the pelting rain
heard his solemn voice. "Evil men must die." He inserted an arrow into the bow and drew the string force-
fully back.

BRAUN WAS THE LAST of X Command to come aboard
the black sailboat. He panted from the swim through
the rough waters.

"Let's get the hell out of here," he yelled to his men
as they stripped out of their wet suits. "This storm's
come up a lot sooner than it was supposed to."

Colonel D. stood stiffly to one side, still clad in his
wet suit. He looked like a man in deep shock. "Zetmer,
get him stripped and below deck," Braun ordered. Then
he noticed Tony and the Kid bound and gagged, lying
on the deck floor. They had life jackets strapped on
tightly, but the packs of MK133 demo charges around
them were unmistakable.

Hampton appeared at his elbow.

"What're you doing with them?" Braun demanded.

Hampton smiled. "I think we can throw them over
and drag them for a while. Then blow them up."

The night was shattered by a cannonball of thunder.

"Throw them in and blow them up now," Braun
said, moving toward the cabin door.

Hampton walked to the immobile youths. Their eyes
grew wide with fear as he approached. "Okay, little
buddies, it's time now." He leered, grabbed Tony first

and threw him over the edge into the high seas. Then Kid. The murderous teenager whined and whimpered through his gag and tried to squirm from Hampton's grip. It was no use. Over he went.

The detonator wire unrolled quickly from its coil on the stern as the boat sailed on, leaving the two boys to bob like corks on a fishing line. George grabbed the hellbox and stood by the cabin, watching his two victims drift farther from the boat. Then he saw the other cruiser sailing straight toward them.

He ran for the stateroom door and pulled it open. "Major Braun!"

The panic in Hampton's voice told Braun something was seriously wrong. He rushed to the door.

"Colonel, they're here. They're coming right at us!"

"Who's here? Who's coming?" Braun said angrily, pushing out the door past Hampton. Again two long veins of lightning streaked the sky, and thunder clapped in the stormy heavens.

Braun saw what was coming—the big SOB cruiser bearing down on them and some crazy guy in the bow.

"Blow the kids up!" He ordered Hampton. "And let's get out of here! They won't use guns. It'll give them away."

Hampton turned back to look at the two victims rolling along the rough waves. Their life jackets barely kept them afloat. He wanted them to know what was happening right to the bitter end.

"Now!" Braun screamed through the rising storm. Hampton pressed the button. Almost.

Whooof! Hampton slammed back against the side of the cabin and the detonator fell from his hands. It clattered onto the deck.

"What the fff..." Braun started yelling at Hampton but stopped. Something was wrong. He was clutching something in his throat and his eyes read pain.

Braun realized what it was. An arrow.

Hampton's hands clawed slowly, trying to pull the wooden missile from his throat. He got the point out of the woodwork behind his neck.

But the head was barbed, and it had already cut through trachea and tissue on the way in.

No trachea, no breath.

Hampton was dead.

Blood burbled out his mouth and from the wound in his throat as he slid down the wall. His body jerked and, as he fell, he sputtered.

Evil men must die.

Whooof! A second arrow flashed and splintered into the cabin door, missing Braun by a foot.

He threw himself onto the deck. He could see the cruiser only a couple hundred feet away.

And he knew exactly what to do.

Blow up the boys. The explosion would divert them. It would also alert the guards at the Sangrino Prison that something was going on out in the bay.

Another arrow landed with a soft firm thud, embedding in the deck behind Braun. He crawled forward on his belly, his eye on the detonator box. The wires were twisted and coiled around Hampton's dead legs.

BILLY TWO COULDN'T GET a clear view of a moving target anymore and now he was just wasting arrows. The waves were so high they pushed the bow of the cruiser up. He couldn't even see the black ship when the cruiser rode the crest of the highest waves.

The storm was quickly turning into a deluge. Visibility was virtually zero. He turned to go back to the bridge where Liam O'Toole was struggling at the helm. Suddenly he thought he heard a voice.

One of his voices.

He stopped to listen. There was no whispering in his ear, no words formed in his head. Around him the storm howled louder. But a sense of urgency invaded him, filling every pore, every atom of his body. He grabbed the railing along the deck and looked out over the water.

Lightning cracked the sky. It was brief, but long enough to see two objects bouncing in the waves off the port side.

Billy Two shucked the bow off his back and shoved it somewhere. He stripped his pants off. Naked as a jaybird save for the belt holding his sheath knife and the bandage around his kidney, he pierced the water in a shallow dive.

He came up in the trough between two waves, held his breath as the breaker crashed over him, forcing him down. His powerful arms swept forward and pulled back up through the turbulent water. For a moment he was disoriented. Then he saw the cruiser loom up behind him and he swam away from it.

Barely three strokes farther on a wave parted like a curtain and revealed a set of terrified eyes staring into his. It was Tony Lopez. Another wave bounced the two of them up in the water. Billy Two reached out and grabbed the life jacket the boy was bound in. Kicking hard to keep his head above water, Starfoot reached out and ripped the tape off Tony's mouth.

The teenager gulped back air and spat out words with panic. "Cut the rope. The rope!"

The Osage warrior didn't understand.

"The rope!" This time Tony screamed. Another wave slammed into them, pushing them together. Billy Two grabbed Tony and pulled him close. He felt around the boy's body until his hands encountered the pack on his back and the line leading from it. Tony was still screaming. Billy Two realized with horror what it was. The shape of a demo pack was unmistakable. So was the feel of primacord. He let go of Tony and pulled his knife from its sheath.

With one hand on the line and his right arm swinging in an arc that was half slash and half swim stroke, he cut the primacord in two.

The great hull of the cruiser loomed high on the crest of a wave over the two swimmers and came down with a mighty crash.

Billy Two reached for Tony Lopez. "I'll swim you to the boat," he screamed over the waves.

"There's another one," Tony shouted back.

A dip in the waves sucked him under. He felt Billy Two's arm reach out and pull his head up. "There's another guy on the line," Tony spluttered and coughed.

Billy Two turned and saw him ten feet away. The terrified eyes of another boy bobbed high up on a wave then disappeared below the surface. He felt his way down to Tony's hands and with one smooth motion of the knife slashed the bonds that held them.

"Can you swim?" he shouted. Tony nodded. Billy Two turned and went for the other one.

He jammed his knife between his teeth and propelled himself forward over the waves with powerful butterfly strokes, taking deep lungfuls of air when the waves cleared before him and smashing through the breakers when they didn't.

He swooped down from a high wave over the floating body of the other boy, grabbing his knife from his teeth. He gripped with his left hand the deadly umbilical while the right slashed the boy free. A giant breaker gathered force, towering mightily overhead. Billy Two took a deep breath and grabbed the boy tightly.

The wave crashed.

The primacord blew.

The entire length went in milliseconds as the electric jolt from the detonator pack flashed through it.

The concussion smashed through the water, but the waves saved them. Working quickly with his knife, Billy Two slashed the explosive pack off and cut the ropes at Kid's wrists. The teenager's body was limp. He was unconscious. Using an over-the-chest carry, Billy Two reached back toward the bow of the cruiser approaching from behind.

Tony had reached the hull of the boat and grabbed a thick rope hanging from the deck. Billy Two took hold of it, gripping his unconscious load tightly.

"Let out some of the rope," he yelled at Tony, backing down the rope so that the forward progress of the boat swept him back toward the stern. Tony followed. Soon they had moved hand over hand down the rope until they were floating off the stern.

"Climb the ladder!" Billy Two shouted.

"I can't. My legs are still tied!"

"Hold him." Billy pushed Kid toward Tony. "Keep his head up." Tony hooked his arm around Kid's neck. Billy Two duck dived.

Tony felt hands go down his legs and the rope at his feet jerk and come loose. Billy Two burst above the surface again and reached for the Kid.

Tony climbed the ladder, slowly and uncertainly. He was weak and disoriented from his ordeal. When he was up, Billy grabbed the rungs. He pulled himself over, grimacing at the dead weight of the unconscious boy.

Tony grabbed Kid when they reached the top of the ladder. They rolled his body over the gunwale, flopping him onto the deck.

Billy Two hauled himself over the edge. He panted hard, his chest heaving mightily. He couldn't talk. The pelting rain stung his skin. He grabbed the unconscious teenager by the neck of his life preserver and dragged him across the heaving deck to the cabin. He waved to Tony to follow.

"Get in there and dry off. Take care of him." He pointed to the Kid. "Is Barrabas on the other boat?" He yelled over the howl of the stern.

Tony shook his head. "No. They went into the fortress. They ambushed them in there and came back with just the prisoner."

Billy Two turned and raced for the bridge.

O'Toole was still struggling with the wheel in the wind, the rain and the savage sea.

"I've lost the other boat," he yelled as Billy Two came under the shelter of the bridge. The rain clattering onto the plastic roof was almost deafening. "Who came aboard?"

"It was Tony Lopez and some other kid. They were thrown overboard," Billy yelled back. "Forget the boat and turn this thing around. Barrabas is still at the fortress."

"Oh shit." O'Toole swung the wheel far to the right, crashing the bow straight into another high roller. Billy Two vanished outside. The fortress was a dark and foreboding silhouette in the blinding rain. The lights inside the walls outlined the ancient fortified ramparts. It was less than half a mile of rough water and high wind away.

But those troubles weren't enough.

A twin-fingered prong of lightning sheeted the sky white. It was followed by a boom of thunder.

This time someone up there on the old stone walls was watching.

Low at first, then rising quickly, another sound ranged above the storm's fury. The howl of a siren.

Billy Two flashed back onto the bridge.

"Shit," O'Toole swore again as the cruiser drove forward through the waves toward the fortress. "What're we doing?"

"We go in beside the fortress and get Barrabas and the others."

Two bright suns suddenly burst into fiery white light at either end of the walls. Giant spots. The stream of light swept through the wind and the rain and zeroed in on the cruiser.

The bridge was filled with white light, causing O'Toole and Starfoot to squint.

"Now what?" O'Toole shouted.

"Same thing!"

"You know what comes next?"

Starfoot knew. The chatter of machine guns. Deadly gossip. Rumors of death.

"We have no grenades, no rockets, no nothing except a couple of rifles." O'Toole inventoried their desperate situation.

"We have this," said Billy Two.

O'Toole looked. The naked Indian held out his bow and a handful of arrows.

For one brief second, O'Toole's hands left the wheel. He buried his face in them.

17

The darkness deep in the bowels of the Spanish fortress was impenetrable. To his right, Barrabas heard Nanos moan and his hands shuffling on the stone floor as he tried to stand up. The mercenary leader moved toward the noise. A light came on.

"It's all right," Nanos said painfully. X Command had forgotten to take his flashlight. The Greek was slowly pushing himself up, shaking his head to clear it. His face was bloody, the right cheek and eye swollen and bruised.

Barrabas took the flashlight.

"Sit for a minute, Alex," he told the merc. "Hayes and I'll get Nate down."

Barrabas held the light as the two men went for Nate Beck, pinned to the wall like a butterfly on a collector's mat. His arms and the sides of his body were drenched with blood from the cruel crucifixion. But he was alive. Slowly and carefully they pulled the knives from the crevices in the wall and lowered him to the floor.

He was unconscious but alive.

Barrabas stripped back his wet suit and tore his undershirt off and into strips. Hayes dug his fingers into the pressure points on the arteries under the armpits to stop the flow of blood. Barrabas tightened tourniquets around Beck's upper arms.

Beck regained consciousness. His eyes were glazed with shock.

"You're okay, Nate," Barrabas told him, his hands moving quickly. "We've stopped the bleeding. We're going to take the knives out. It's going to hurt."

He took a useless mouthpiece from the ruined scuba assembly and tore the rubber pad off it. He stuck it in the wounded man's mouth between his teeth. "Bite," he said.

"Okay?" Hayes asked.

Barrabas nodded. He held the tourniquet as tight as he could. The black man leaned over Beck and gripped one of the knives. He pulled. The bloody thing came up with a big burble of blood. Nate groaned and twisted.

Nanos held the flashlight and wiped the wounded man's forehead with the remains of Barrabas's T-shirt.

"One more," Hayes muttered softly. They repeated the performance. Nate passed out again.

Barrabas dipped his finger in Beck's mouth to remove the rubber plug before he choked on it. "If we get him some proper first aid, he'll live."

"How the hell are any of us going to get out of here?" Nanos put it very succinctly.

The underwater swim was out of the question.

Barrabas focused on the plans of the prison that he'd studied in Florida. He'd memorized as much of the layout as he could.

"I'll get us out of here," he told them. "First we have to get him up that ladder. Tie his wrists to his belt. I'll go first. Hayes, you and Nanos hand him up to me."

Barrabas took two of the M-16s and Beck's extra mags. He climbed up the ladder and through the open door. Hayes gently hoisted the unconscious soldier over his shoulder and with one hand on the rungs started up the ladder. At the top, Barrabas slipped his hands between Nate's immobilized arms and torso and pulled him back onto the floor behind him. Hayes came through quickly.

Barrabas stuck his head into the tunnel to call to Nanos. "Bring the explosives and the rope. On the floor near the equipment." A minute later Alex was up. They had everything they needed.

"At the T in the corridor we turn left instead of right," Barrabas instructed them. "That'll lead to the utility plant. There are windows facing out onto the bay. We might have to blow a hole to make one bigger, but we can drop down to the walkway below. When we all get out we go for one of the Cuban gunboats. Ready?"

"The third one," said Hayes. Barrabas looked at him questioningly. "The third boat," Hayes repeated. "Not the first two."

Hayes lifted Beck gently over his shoulder and handed his M-16 to Nanos. Barrabas started forward toward the dim glow of the light that marked the corridor.

It was a long shot that they could make it. If they got onto the walkway and stuck close to the walls, the guards on the ramparts above couldn't get them without shooting straight down. But then they were talking about hijacking a gunboat. Long odds. Especially with a wounded man in tow. But they weren't going to leave anyone behind. And they weren't going to stop trying until all possibilities of escape were exhausted.

And the possibilities ended only one way. By dying.

From far away, deep inside the fortress, something else started. At first it seemed like a mere vibration from a strong wind. Then it grew. The awareness hit each man in the stomach like a solid punch from an iron fist.

A siren.

The gig was up.

"Move it!" Barrabas yelled. Nanos and Hayes started running. By the time they got to the T, they could hear the sound of booted feet stampeding down the steps from the upper cell blocks.

Lots of them.

"Go left," Barrabas shouted, "and keep going straight. I'll catch up." Hayes and Nanos left him. He took the rucksack of explosives off his back and pulled out the hellbox.

He looked briefly and found the wires Nate had left hanging up to the plastic explosives overhead. The man wasn't an explosives expert, but he'd done a thorough job of tamping the volatile plastique into the overhead brickwork. Barrabas hooked the wires into the hellbox and started back down the left-hand corridor, letting the wire out as he went. The stomping footsteps from the onrushing Cuban soldiers grew louder.

The first one turned the corner far down the corridor. He had friends right behind. He saw Barrabas and shouted. Barrabas kept backing away. He watched them bring up their guns as they ran forward. He could almost see their knuckles whiten as their fingers closed on the triggers.

He pushed the button.

Chinks of flying stone and masonry pinged into Barrabas as he turned and threw himself onto the floor. A couple of fair-sized rocks slugged into his back. The corridor was dense with smoke and thick clouds of dust. He could barely breathe. The shouts and cries from behind the pile of debris indicated that the surprised Cubans had taken the worst of it. The fortress was old. Big stones were still falling from the ruined ceiling and disappearing in the gray cloud of dust.

Barrabas was up and running.

The sound of humming machinery grew louder as he approached the end of the corridor and passed through a metal door into the utility room. He could make out rows of arcane machinery, pumps and electrical devices.

"Colonel, over here!" Hayes was calling to him from the far wall. "You've got the explosives. We have to blow the bars off this window to get out. But look what's coming in!"

Barrabas looked through the narrow window set waist-high in the thick stone wall. A few hundred yards offshore, barely visible through the wind-driven rain, was the most welcome sight he'd ever seen. The cruiser coming in full tilt for the walkway below. He watched as the water ten feet in front of the boat erupted in a line of miniature geysers. The sound of machine-gun fire came from the walls overhead.

"I hope they make it," he said.

"So do I," Hayes seconded.

The black warrior pulled another two-and-a-half-pound block of plastique out and was molding it along the bars where they were set in the thick stone.

"How much do you need for the walls?" Barrabas demanded.

"With this much brick, all of it. And this is all we got."

"I need a little." The colonel grabbed a piece. "Just enough to blow some fuses."

BILLY TWO DISAPPEARED from the bridge, leaving O'Toole to his suicide mission. He was running the cruiser on an oblique angle to the walkway, and hoping like hell there weren't any rocks underwater. He figured if he came in sideways at this speed, the cruiser would need a new paint job. If he went in bow first, he'd need a new boat.

The walls of the fortress loomed higher through the blowing sheets of rain. Then he heard the first round of machine-gun fire and the heaving water erupted in little whirlpools. The bullets went wide. But he had a feeling the Cubans would have the azimuth adjusted second time around.

Billy Two reappeared, this time carrying O'Toole's equipment bag. He hauled out a block of plastic explosives and quickly began taping a chunk around the shaft of his arrow. Then he embedded a delay blasting cap. He stood by the door to the deck and inserted the arrow in the bow. Holding it in place, he lit the fuse.

He stepped outside. It was raining very hard, lead as well as water.

The machine gun chattered on again. This time the bullets came home, chunking into the wood along the hull. Another fifty feet and the boat would be under the walls and out of the line of fire. Billy Two drew the bowstring and aimed the sizzling missile higher than the top of the ramparts. He let it go. The arrow left the bow with a firm twang and soared like an orange sputtering rocket high into the dark wet rain.

Billy Two darted under the shelter of the bridge.

"Down, Starfoot!" O'Toole shouted. He was hunched behind the steering wheel. Billy went down. This time the machine gun was dead on. Bullets whammed through the plastic roof and the windows and chunked into the wooden sides.

Then they heard the rain-muffled explosion.

Billy Two popped his head up. He let out a blood-curdling war whoop.

"It's clear. I got it!" he shouted.

O'Toole came up. Bits of debris were still falling in flames from the ramparts where once a machine gun and gunners had been. The exploding arrow had taken out one of the bright spotlights, too.

Liam adjusted his course to take the boat in along the walkway.

Then the bullets started coming from up front.

There was another gun on the other side.

The windscreen above the control panel shattered and bullets chunked around them. O'Toole roared with pain. His left hand was hit and spurting blood. He rammed it back onto the wheel and ducked down again. Billy was squatting with another arrow and more explosives.

Then the giant klieg light on the ramparts went out.

"Light!" Billy Two yelled. "I need a light. I can't see what I'm doing!"

O'Toole tried to look through the darkness, but he couldn't. The night was total again. He stood up. This time he war whooped. "Yahooo! Billy Two!"

"Light. I need some light!"

"No, Starfoot," O'Toole yelled back above the storm. "That's our boys. They're in there somewhere. And they just turned out the lights!"

More machine-gun fire rapped out from the darkened walls. This time their aim was off. Bullets chunked into the hull and deck and smashed a port window.

O'Toole used his right hand to steer hard against the wind and waves. His left was bleeding badly. The blood was slippery on the wheel.

The walkway was coming up fast. O'Toole pulled the wheel to his left to straighten the boat parallel to the sides of the fortress. It seemed like the rolling waves smashing against the rock walls were going to do the rest for him.

They were under the protection of the wall, but not for long. Troops on the ramparts would start picking them off with direct downward shots. And where the hell was Barrabas?

An explosion high up on the stone wall blew out a fury of rock and smoke. That's where!

Billy Two war whooped at the top of his voice. O'Toole joined in. The cruiser hit the stone edge of the walkway with a grinding lurch, pushed by the driving waves that washed up over the deck. The impact knocked both men against the side of the bridge.

Through the howling storm they both heard hard pops of rifles and bullets chipping into stone. The guards on the ramparts were shooting down at them like fish in a barrel.

"Stay! I go!" Billy Two leaped from the bridge to the deck and from the deck to the walkway. He left his bow behind. This time he grabbed an M-16.

O'Toole couldn't keep the boat in one place. He had it in neutral, but the rolling action of the waves picked the cruiser up and shoved it against the stone walls over and over again. He could hear the fiberglass and wood crunching and bending. A few more hard knocks and the thing was going to break up. "Please hurry," he prayed softly, using the weight of his body along his right arm to keep the wheel from spinning out of control.

Billy Two hit the walkway with his bare feet and ran swiftly until he came to the rubble from the explosion. The tail end of the rope dropped from above. Bullets pinged against the stone wall, knocking shards of rock against his skin. The Cubans were still shooting down at them. In just a minute a whole army was going to come sweeping around the corner of the fortress and bear straight down on him. He just knew it.

A pair of feet suddenly appeared at the end of the window. They were followed by legs. Someone was coming down the rope.

Starfoot flattened himself against the fortification and aimed the M-16 straight up, squinting against the pouring rain. He fired off a mag, spraying the bullets back and forth along the top of the wall and into the air. It stopped the Cuban guards for the moment. He reached for his mag belt to get a fresh one. Then he realized he was still stark naked. He didn't have a mag belt. He didn't have any bullets at all.

Nanos hit the stone pavement beside him.

"Hey, Alex, I need a mag."

Nanos looked at the naked Indian. He didn't ask questions. He just threw him the mag.

Claude Hayes was at the top of the rope. Barrabas passed Nate Beck through to him. The bullets from above started up again.

Nanos and Starfoot joined forces, sending rivers of hot lead back up through the rain to the tops of the walls. Hayes started down the rope with Beck over his shoulder. It was slow going.

Starfoot and Nanos jumped erratically back and

forth farther up the walkway. The orange tracers from their guns drew the Cubans' attention away from the men on the rope.

Hayes hit the bottom. Barrabas was on his way down. Chips of rock exploded from the stone walls, stinging Billy Two and Nanos. With one hand on the rope and his feet crossed to slow his descent and stop the burn, Barrabas raised his M-16 and fired on the way down. A heavy gust of wind caught him, shoving him hard against the stone wall. Serious sandpaper. He felt the skin of his face and arm peeling away and the hard rain stinging the raw flesh.

But he kept pouring the lead up at the ramparts. The guard tower shut up for a moment. Barrabas hit the ground. No one stopped to say hello.

Nanos raced ahead and leaped across the space between the boat and wall as the waves pulled the cruiser away from the edge. He ran to the bridge to give O'Toole an experienced hand at the wheel.

Then the army came.

Cuban soldiers began pouring through the rain around the corner of the fortress.

Hayes was waiting for the waves to bring the boat closer. There was a six-foot gap of greedy water, and he still had Nate Beck over his shoulder.

"Jump!" Barrabas yelled, running full speed from the Cuban army. "Jump!"

Billy Two appeared at Hayes's side.

"I can't do it myself," Hayes said. "He's too heavy."

"Give me half and back up to the wall," Starfoot yelled. He grabbed Nate's body and shifted some of the weight over his shoulder. The two mercs backed up for a running start. They ran. A wave picked the boat up, pushing it back toward them as they got to the edge. A flying leap took them across the narrowed gap and they landed on their feet with Nate between them.

"Take him below," Hayes yelled. "I'll go for the bridge."

Still on the walkway, Barrabas was giving the Cuban army M-16 hell.

His mag emptied.

Just in time for Billy Two to pick up the slack.

The Indian squeezed the trigger and sent bullets for a walk. The Cuban army ran.

On the bridge, Nanos took over the wheel and rammed the gear into Forward. The boat moved along the walkway toward the colonel. He steered left to counter the heavy wave action that forced the boat against the stone sides of the fortress.

A falling wave dragged the cruiser into its trough, pulling it six feet from the shore. The gap was widening. Barrabas gave it a running jump, throwing his weight forward.

His feet half landed on the edge of the deck with the waves rocking the boat down. He stretched his arms out to throw his weight forward. It wasn't working. He tipped back into the waves. Starfoot's hand reached out and grabbed his. He jerked once, let go and went back to working the M-16.

It was enough to catapult Barrabas forward onto the slippery deck. He twisted to land on his backside.

Nanos turned the wheel sharply left and headed the cruiser out into the bay.

He gritted his teeth and gripped the wheel as if his

own strength would force the cruiser to cut faster through the rolling waves of the storm-tossed sea.

The waves were pocked by sheets of rain and it still wasn't all water. Nanos could hear fire from the other machine guns. They were shooting blindly into the darkness from the high walls of the fortress. The cruiser was moving back into range.

Suddenly Billy Two was back on the bridge behind him, doing his trick with the arrow again.

"Gun it!" the Osage yelled, drawing the bowstring back furiously. The arrow soared through the deluge.

An orange explosion lit the stone walls of the Sangrino just above the ramparts.

It didn't make it.

But it shut them up.

"Hurry!" Starfoot yelled again, his hands working overtime with another lump of plastique and another arrow. On the deck of the cruiser, Barrabas and Hayes were sending rapid streams of autofire skating along the walkway. The Cuban army made their retreat around the corner of the fortress.

But the machine gun up high was back in business.

Chunk, chunk, chunk!

Bullets splintered into the cruiser. Nanos yelped and slapped his arm as a fiberglass shard pierced his skin.

Starfoot was ready again. He drew. He shot. The arrow flew. It went over the ramparts. There was a slight pause. The rain might have put out the fuse.

Lead messengers from the MGs were knocking again.

Chunk, chunk, boom! Another orange explosion. This time it came from behind the walls. Right on, Starfoot!

The dark prison grew smaller as the cruiser ate up distance. The veils of heavy rain obscured the target for both sides.

Rifle chatter stopped, giving way to the howling wind and blowing water. But the mercs weren't out of trouble yet.

Another sound cut the noise of the storm.

"Oh, shit," Nanos moaned. "They're bringing the navy."

The cruiser still had a third of the distance of the bay to cross before open water, and the PT boats could at least match the cruiser's speed. At least.

"Just keep driving!" Hayes called to him. Barrabas came up the steps onto the bridge. The side of his head was cut and coated with blood, and his right arm was scraped raw to the muscle. He didn't seem to notice.

"How's it going, Alex?"

"Just barely, Colonel. It's like they say at the races. Don't look back. You'll see someone gaining on you."

Hayes joined them. "Go ahead, Alex. Look back."

Alex turned.

There were four of them. Great dark shadows cutting across the water. Each had a single spotlight for a cyclops eye at the bow.

"Claude, why're you making my life miserable?"

"Just watch, Alex."

Boom! The bow of the closest boat blew into the air with bits of fiery metal flying off in all directions.

Boom! The second boat blew as well.

"Stopped dead!" Hayes said happily.

"Mainly dead," Barrabas commented. "Congratulations. I figured you planted explosives on the hulls of a few boats when we went into the fortress. Do you have any plans for the other two?"

"My turn now, Colonel," Nanos said. He turned just in time to see the high rocky cliffs guarding the entrance to the bay loom up overhead.

Sheltered between the cliffs, the water was momentarily calmer. The cruiser zipped through and smashed head-on into a mother of a breaker. The impact was sharp enough to throw all the mercs back against the wall of the bridge, grabbing for something to hold on to. Nanos gritted and held the wheel as the tow force against the rudder tried to seize control.

Hayes grabbed half the wheel and the two men strained to push it around. They kept the cruiser running in a straight line out from the shore.

The two remaining PT boats soared through the bay entrance and into the open water right on their tail.

"Now!" Nanos shouted.

The two men quickly pushed the wheel all the way to the right, turning the boat in a wide arc and heading it back toward the bay. The two PT boats were coming right at them now, a quarter of a mile across the stormy waves.

Boom, boom!

Fire on the water!

Twice again explosions lit the stormy night. The PT boats hit the line of mines the mercs had removed from the bay entrance and strung out from shore.

"Bye bye, Cubans," Nanos whooped.

The two mercs at the wheel turned the boat around and aimed for Florida.

For a moment the men were silent, watching the sheets of rain flap and flutter outside the bullet-smashed windshield. Water dripped through holes in the plastic roof.

"I can take it now," said Hayes. He meant the helm. "What the hell is all this sticky stuff." He wiped his hands on his pants.

"Blood," said Nanos.

"O'Toole got a bullet in his left hand," Starfoot told them.

Barrabas looked from soldier to soldier. They were a mess. All except Hayes had taken an injury somehow, somewhere. Three of them were in bloody wet suits, torn and slashed from action. Billy Two was still stark naked except for the knife belt and a bloody bandage across his kidneys. They were all soaking wet, and rainwater dripped onto their heads from bullet holes in the plastic roof.

"Where's O'Toole?" the colonel asked.

"He went down to take care of Beck," said Starfoot. "And Colonel, Tony Lopez is down there with some other kid. I dragged them out of the water. X Command threw them overboard tied to TNT twinpacks. I don't know who the other guy is, but they're both okay."

"Dumb kids," Barrabas muttered.

"Hey," Hayes protested. "We were kids, too, once. And dumb."

"No. Not dumb. Hotheaded, but not dumb."

The sea was actually rougher than it had been inside the sheltered bay. The cruiser bucked and lurched back and forth on the tops of waves. And the force of the rain was unabated. But it was quieter now that the battle was over and they were out. Wounded, exhausted, but alive and each of them in one piece.

"I'm going below. The rest of you clean up. Hayes, I'll relieve you when I'm finished with Tony Lopez."

Barrabas went back into the rain and descended to the

deck. Nanos, Starfoot and Hayes rode in silence for a while. Hayes spoke first.

"The colonel knows war like he was born to it. But he sure don't know teenage kids."

Starfoot nodded.

"But you got to admit," said Nanos, "Lopez's kid brother sure turned out to be a pain in the ass."

18

Tony and the Kid were alone in the cabin. For a long time, they eyed each other in complete silence. Farther forward, in the bow section, O'Toole took care of Nate Beck's wounds. Kid spoke first. His voice was weak. "What are you going to tell them?"

Tony turned away and looked off into space. His eyes were filled with anger.

"Please," Kid pleaded.

Tony looked at him again. The bravado was gone. In its place was a frightened, weak-looking, pale, gangly kid who had gotten way out of his league and been burned. Tony was in much the same position. But at least his pretensions hadn't been as bad. He felt sorry for the Kid.

"The truth."

"I didn't know, honestly I didn't. If I had known they were the bad guys I wouldn't have gone on their side, I swear."

Tony eyed him silently, not commenting.

"I'm sorry I got you in trouble. Really."

"Yeah?" Tony was doubtful.

"Uh-huh." Kid nodded. "Don't tell them. Okay?"

Tony eyed Kid silently and coldly.

The cruiser lurched in a high wave. A flare of lightning whitened the sky outside the portholes and thunder cracked. The door to the cabin swung back. Rain and wind invaded.

The lightning outlined the big man standing in the doorway. The blood from his face and arms mixed with rain and trickled in red rivulets down his clothing and skin. His eyes glinted darkly.

For a moment he didn't speak.

He slammed the door shut behind him. The sound of the wind and rain faded. The boat heaved from side to side on its journey through the storm. Barrabas planted his legs apart and stood arms akimbo. His brow was curled in anger. He studied the two boys.

"Hello, Tony," he finally said. Tony's head dropped. He couldn't look Barrabas in the face. He felt the mercenary leader's blue eyes drilling into him.

Neither could the Kid, who shrunk back against the seat as if he might not be noticed. He was. Barrabas flicked his eyes that way. Kid felt them.

"And who are you?"

"K-K-Kid. My name's Kid. I wanted...to join the mercenaries. Like he did." He motioned toward Tony. "I got sucked in, too. Isn't that right, Tony?"

Tony didn't answer.

"Is that right, Tony?" Barrabas demanded.

Tony looked at Kid, then up at Barrabas. Then his eyes rested on the Kid. "That's right," he said grimly.

Barrabas studied the two boys for a moment. "Either of you got any idea what's gone on tonight?"

Kid and Tony looked at each other, then at the floor, waiting for the other to speak first. Tony broke the silence.

"Some of it. I guess I really screwed up. They kept

talking about their enemy. I didn't know that meant you...until the end.''

"Any idea where they are now?''

Both teenagers shook their heads and stared morosely off into space.

"It's not likely they'll go to their beach house on Anna Maria,'' Barrabas said.

Neither Kid nor Tony responded at first. Then Tony's head rose and for the first time he spoke directly to Barrabas.

"The yacht,'' he said.

"What?''

"The yacht. They're taking the yacht to a marina at Bradenton Beach. They're taking Colonel D. there. I heard Braun say so. Yes, that's it.'' Tony was suddenly excited. He'd stumbled upon a little fact that meant nothing to him a few hours earlier. Now it was everything. It was his chance to make up a little for what he'd done.

"It's true,'' he assured the cold-eyed warrior at the cabin door. "I swear. We were driving over the causeway onto Anna Maria. We went by the marina. Braun and Zetmer both looked at the yacht. And they said that when they got the colonel back from Cuba, that's where they'd take him. To meet someone who was going to give them money or something. I stopped listening, because it wasn't important then.''

Barrabas nodded slowly. What Tony was saying made sense. Another missing piece of the puzzle. All that remained was to put a face on it.

"So you two wanted to be mercenaries,'' Barrabas said to them, his voice softening.

Tony nodded. "Yeah. I'm sorry now. It's...not what it's cracked up to be.''

"You, too?" Barrabas said to the Kid.

The teenager looked resentful. "Someone's got to do it. They're letting the scum out all over the place. Some-one's got to stand up and fight."

Barrabas looked at him, for a moment not knowing what to say. He'd heard it all before. It was the kind of knee-jerk thing said by people who didn't think. In real life it was much more complicated than all that, and he didn't really want to think about it.

"What's that got to do with you?" he asked the Kid.

"When the scum are on the loose someone's got to go after them. To fight against them. Get rid of them. If they're scum they have to die."

"No man has the right to make that kind of judg-ment," Barrabas said angrily. "No man. And anyone who thinks that way is really no better than the scum he wants to get rid of. You can't make yourself sound right because you set yourself up as a judge and jury. It doesn't make you right. It makes you a killer. Any way you look at it, you're just a killer." Barrabas turned to go.

"Isn't that what you are?"

Thunder clapped. Barrabas swung back and glared at Kid again. His eyes had steel rims and glowed, his white hair lit the darkness and his lips rested in something be-tween a snarl and a scowl. "You think it's great, don't you? It's not. You've got a fantasy in your head and it's nothing like what it really is all about. Stick with your fantasy. Leave the real world to me. I'm the who you didn't have a choice. I'm just a tool cast from a certain die. It's my fate to be a killer. Do you think I've never wanted another destiny?"

Lightning flared and thunder boomed again.

The door slammed open, admitting the howl of wind and rain.

"Yeah. I'm a killer. And if I have to, I'll kill you."

Barrabas turned and was gone. Kid's mouth dropped open in terror and surprise. Tony stared at him with eyes dark and cold.

BY SUNRISE, when the cruiser had entered Florida water, the storm had vanished as rapidly as it had arrived. The morning sun unfurled its blanket of pinkish gold over the calm gulf waters. Palms along the far shore swayed lazily in the new daylight, and pelicans swooped for their breakfast over the surface of the gently rolling sea.

"Is this the same ocean we were on last night?" Nanos said to Hayes as the black man steered parallel to the ocean.

Hayes just smiled.

They heard the cabin door open and close below. Barrabas walked up to the bridge.

"So Colonel?" Hayes asked. Each of them had managed a small amount of sleep, with Hayes and Nanos spelling each other at the helm.

"There's a fishing wharf about a quarter of a mile down from the marina. We'll dock there. Nate's got to get to a doctor soon, and Billy Two's wound is more serious than he's letting on. Also O'Toole's. He can't use his hand. The bullet went right through the palm. I ordered the three of them to get to a doctor the moment we dock. That leaves three of us. If their yacht is at the marina, there can't be many more than a half dozen of X Command around."

"And we'll have the element of surprise," said Hayes.

"Two to one." Nanos mused. "It's about our usual odds."

"I just want to get this all straightened out this morning. And settle once and for all with Braun, X Command and Colonel D."

"What about Tony and the Kid?" Hayes asked.

"They'll stay put," Barrabas said evenly. "Until we get back."

THE LONG, SLEEK black-hulled yacht floated gently by the marina wharf. An equally long, sleek black limousine idled a hundred feet away on the shore road.

Inside the stateroom of the yacht, the well-dressed man from the senator's office paced across the polished wood floors. The heels of his shoes clicked slowly and deliberately with each step, as if they counted time.

Major Braun stood nearby. The major wasn't happy, nor was the visitor.

But it didn't bother Colonel D., who sat on a cushioned bench by a porthole and stared wordlessly off into space. His eyes were vacant, without feeling, expression or thought. He blinked occasionally. Otherwise, he didn't move.

"So this is what you've brought me?" asked the visitor. "A vegetable. This is what I'm paying you for?"

"Get off it," Braun said sharply. "We got him from the prison. How were we supposed to know what they did to him inside? Look at his arms. It looks like they used him for a chemical storage tank."

The visitor continued to pace, peering absentmindedly out the different portholes as he moved around the stateroom. He walked over to Colonel D.

"Maybe we can train him to do tricks," he said. "Hello, Colonel. Are you all right?"

The colonel didn't move. The visitor bent down to speak directly into the colonel's ear.

"Colonel wanna cracker?" he asked in a singsong voice.

The colonel blinked.

The visitor mocked surprise. "Well, well, give the man a cracker, Major Braun. He just responded."

"Perhaps with treatment . . ."

"And perhaps not." This time the visitor's words came closer to a shout. "In the meantime, what the hell are we supposed to do with him? What do we say when people start asking questions? I'm not pleased at all, Major Braun." He kept his back turned to the X Command leader and continued to pace the room, peering through the round windows.

"At least we accomplished that much. We got rid of Barrabas once and for all."

"Oh, did you, Major Braun?" the visitor said, arrested momentarily at a window that looked down the long wharf. "Then, pray tell me who that is coming toward the boat?"

THE GUY WHO OWNED the car rental franchise in Bradenton Beach had it made the day that he rented out two cars to a bunch of big guys who pounded on his door half an hour before he was even open.

Hayes and Barrabas each drove one back to the cruiser. They carried Beck from below deck and laid him on the back seat. Beck's condition was stable and the bleeding had stopped. But he needed medical attention quickly to patch together torn muscle and close the wound. As did Liam O'Toole. The bullet had gone straight through his palm and taken some meat with it. His hand was splintered, bandaged, extremely painful and useless for fighting. Billy Two showed no pain nor any sign of discomfort from the wound near his left kidney. But it still hadn't stopped bleeding.

Barrabas didn't give them a choice.

"You said you know a doctor in Tampa who'll keep his mouth shut for the right price. So go there and that's an order. Alex and Claude and I will take care of things here."

As soon as the car carrying the three men was out of sight, Barrabas went below deck. Tony and the Kid had stretched out to sleep on the cushioned seats along the sides of the cabin. Now they were awake.

"We have some business to take care of," he told them. "We'll be back. I'm ordering you both to stay put. If you don't, there'll be hell to pay. You've both caused enough problems already."

The teenagers nodded.

The three remaining mercs stocked up on spare mags. They wore baggy green bush jackets to cover the bulk and hide the M-16s. It was a good disguise. They were dressed much like the old men who had come down to the wharf to sit in the warm sun with their fishing lines out in the water, heads back and eyes closed.

A few minutes later, Barrabas, Hayes and Nanos arrived at the marina in the second car. Barrabas noticed the limousine idling at the foot of the wharf.

Out in the water, at the other end, the black yacht floated at anchor.

Hayes turned the car around and aimed the tail end at the sailboat.

"Ready?" Barrabas asked. Hayes nodded. "Go!"

Hayes floored it. The tires spun briefly then caught and the car rocketed in reverse down the long wooden wharf. The yacht grew bigger, fast.

"Oh, shit," Nanos moaned. The car had about five feet to go before it came to the end of the wharf and went straight onto the deck of the yacht. And Hayes still wasn't slowing down. Barrabas's hand tightened on the door handle. Hayes braked. The car screeched, bucked and bounced on its springs, and the taillights kissed the edge of the boat. The mercs jumped out and went over the side onto the empty deck.

There was an entrance below deck at the bow, and one midship. Nanos ran for the bow while Barrabas booted open the midship door. Hayes aimed his M-16 as the door flew back.

Nanos hadn't made it very far when a heavy green tarpaulin on the bridge suddenly erupted.

Two men appeared with autorifles.

Barrabas aimed. The trigger tickled his finger. He saw tracers. His finger itched. He let loose a 3-round burst. Scratch one bad guy.

Hayes stitched the second out. They slammed against each other, back to bloody back. One collapsed in a tangle of tarpaulin. The other wobbled slowly like a falling tree. He fell, plunging with a dead thud onto the deck.

But Nanos caught lead.

"Check him out and cover the bow!" Barrabas shouted at Hayes. The black man bent over the Greek.

Barrabas slipped through the stateroom door, his finger still tight on the trigger of his autorifle. He saw the door leading forward in the ship close as he entered, and he saw Colonel D. sitting on a couch staring off into space.

"Behind you." It was his instinct shouting. He ducked.

The stock of a rifle swung hard and clipped the back of his head. He felt warm blood trickle down his neck as he swung around.

Zetmer, the stocky, muscular man, drove the butt forward into Barrabas's stomach. An ordinary man would have lost his wind.

Barrabas was no ordinary man. He arched in with the blow, the hard muscles of his stomach shielding his guts and diaphragm. But Zetmer had jumped forward, his eyes lusting to kill. The butt of the rifle swung again. This time it came down hard on Barrabas's forearm, knocking his rifle down.

"I'm going to kill," Zetmer whispered savagely. "Man from hell." He threw his rifle down and socked Barrabas in the face with a right, following with a left.

Zetmer's chest heaved. He came in for more blows.

The man was good.

Barrabas was better.

He caught Zetmer's fist with his left arm and deflected it, following up with a solid punch to the gut with his right. This time it was Zetmer's turn to suck air. Barrabas was too fast to let him.

His big hands grabbed the sides of Zetmer's face. He kneed upward and rammed the commando's face down. The deadly dance began. Knee to nose; nose to knee. Bone crunched. Blood spurted.

He grabbed Zetmer's hair and pulled his head up. Zetmer's hands dropped and swung at his sides. All Barrabas could see were the whites of his eyes. Blood poured down the front of the body. He'd driven the nose right back into Zetmer's brain. No more Zetmer.

He threw the body back against the wall, grabbed his rifle and went for the forward cabins.

There were two of them, both empty. Suddenly, he heard the drone of a speedboat pulling up beside the yacht.

Barrabas ran up to the deck

THE SOBs HAD JUST LEFT the cruiser when the Kid started moving around, fidgety and restless. He cast occasional glances at Tony.

"What's the matter with you?" Tony asked.

Kid shrugged. "Nothing. 'Cept your friend Barrabas."

"What's the matter with Barrabas?"

"Thinks he's tough."

"He is."

"Ah, you get sucked in by everyone."

"Yeah. I guess I do. I saved your neck, didn't I?"

Kid turned to look at Tony. "Where you figure they keep the guns on board here?"

Tony looked back. He felt trouble brewing. "What are you talking about?" He moved in front of the Kid.

"I'm talking about action. Now get out of my way."

"Uh-uh, Kid. You're not going anywhere."

The Kid tried to push Tony out of the way. Tony grabbed his arms. The two boys joined in combat, tipping onto the floor where they rolled back and forth in a contest for power.

Kid was taller, but Tony was stronger. He twisted around until he was behind Kid and then he put the

Kid's neck in an armlock. The Kid struggled, trying to pull his arm away, but Tony was too strong for him.

"Like I said, Kid. This time you're not going anywhere. And when Barrabas gets back, I tell the whole story."

Kid stopped struggling. He took his left hand away from Tony's arm and began reaching across the floor. Tony didn't notice.

"Yeah? And what's he going to do?" Kid demanded.

"Something. I don't know. But something."

Kid's hand gripped the diver's weight belt he had seen under the bench. Slowly he pulled it toward him.

"Uh-uh, Tony Lopez. 'Cause Major Braun's going to take care of Barrabas. Barrabas is a wimp. Braun's the tough guy."

"What are you talking about? They tried to kill us."

"That was Hampton. Braun didn't know. If Braun was there he would have stopped it."

"You're crazy."

"Uh-uh." Kid swung the lead-studded weight belt as hard as he could into Tony's face. Blood poured from the split skin on his forehead. His arm loosened just enough. Kid ripped it away from his neck and swung out of the lock.

Their positions were reversed. Tony struggled. Kid still had the weight belt. He hit Tony twice on the back of the head and the struggle ended. Tony was unconscious.

It took Kid only a few minutes to find a locker under the control panel on the bridge and even less time to smash the lock off with a fire ax. Inside he found what he wanted—an M-16 with a silencer and a few extra mags.

Tony was regaining consciousness by the time the Kid went below deck. He grabbed some rope and tied him up. "I'll be back for you," he said and left.

With the M-16 under his jacket he stepped onto the wharf and walked. He was getting high again on the thrill of the sport. He remembered how it had all begun just a day ago: blowing away Wally Garvis and his mother and brother; the flight through the back alleys in his blood-spattered clothing; the feeling that his feet would never touch the ground again, that he could fly.

Barrabas's words floated into his head. "No one has the right to judge. Make any excuse you want, but you're just a killer." Let's put it this way, he thought. I won't kill unless I have to, but I'm looking for an excuse.

Just then ne found the excuse he was looking for. A fisherman sat in a speedboat sorting out his tackle box.

"Hi," said the Kid with a big friendly smile.

The middle-aged man looked up. "Hello there, son. How are you today?"

"I'm great, Gramps. I got something for you."

"Oh? What's that?"

"This." He pulled the M-16 out of his jacket and fired. Skin and blood exploded across the man's chest. He tipped forward and fell face first into the water. Kid jumped into the speedboat. He threw the tackle box after the body. The water next to the boat was red with blood.

A moment later he had the motor started. He ran the boat slowly up beside the cruiser. Then he went inside to get Tony. The marina where the X Command yacht was moored was only a few minutes away. If he hurried, he might be able to warn them.

If not, at least he had a hostage

WHEN BARRABAS GOT TO THE DECK the sound of the speedboat was loud, almost under the yacht. He ran toward the bow on the side away from the wharf and looked down over the edge. The speedboat pulled away from the yacht and sped out into the gulf. It was a reflex for him to bring up the M-16, his finger tightening against the steel trigger. But even as his body reacted, his mind knew it was too late. They were out of range.

The boat grew tinier in the distance. Braun had made his escape good. And the Kid was at the wheel.

"Colonel!" He heard Hayes calling and it sounded urgent.

The black man was helping Nanos sit up against the cabin housing. The Greek had taken 5.56mm in and out on an angle through the side of his chest. The exit wound was missing a big chunk of meat.

Barrabas moved beside them.

"Colonel, look down the wharf," Hayes said quickly.

A man in a suit was walking rapidly toward the black limousine.

"He came off the boat. Want me to shoot him?"

The escaping man looked back over his shoulder at the men on the yacht. Barrabas took a snapshot with his mind's camera. It was a face he was going to remember.

"No. Let him go. I'll deal with him later. Right now I want Braun."

"The beach house?" Hayes suggested.

"Maybe. How're you doing, Alex?"

"Dumb fuckers," the wounded man muttered. "I'll blow their fucking heads off."

"We already did, Alex," said Hayes.

"Let's get him in the car and you guys get the hell out of here."

"I can walk," Nanos insisted. They helped him to his feet and started toward the car.

"What about Colonel D.?"

"Leave him. He won't go anywhere. He's still in shock."

Hayes headed around to the driver's door and climbed in as Barrabas helped Nanos in the other side.

From the highway that ran along the shore, the mercs heard sirens. Barrabas looked up. A half mile away a couple of police cars with cherries flashing were coming fast, probably coming for them.

"Looks like someone heard shots," Barrabas said grimly.

"I'll make sure they're off you're tail, Colonel," Hayes promised.

The engine roared to life and the car zipped down the wharf. Strolling fishermen leaped for their boats.

Barrabas grabbed his gun. He was after Braun. But there was something else far more important. The original cause. Tony Lopez. What had they done to him now? There was a speedboat moored a dozen yards down the wharf. He went for it.

BARRABAS STOOD IN THE CABIN of the cruiser. There was blood on the floor and blood on the weight belt nearby. But no sign of Tony Lopez. And the Kid had found one of their M-16s.

There was only one thing he could do—cross his fingers and try the beach house.

It took him ten minutes in the stolen speedboat to drive up the channel between Anna Maria Island and the mainland until he came to a thin divide in the island that allowed through traffic to the gulf. A few minutes later he saw the beachfront park that doubled as lovers' lane by night. He brought the speedboat straight up onto the shore until the propeller caught in sand and the engine stalled. He jumped out and ran through the foot-high waves onto the beach.

The pine forest was to his left. He approached the beach house that way. When he had a view of the building through the evenly planted rows of trees, he stopped to study it. It looked deserted.

Treading softly on the sandy forest floor he walked slowly on from tree to tree until he came to the edge of the forest. There was twenty feet of open space to the ruined doorway. Still no sign of life.

He'd have to chance it.

Then he heard noises behind him. Footsteps and a metallic click. Uh-uh. Looked like he wouldn't have to bother.

"Sneaking up on someone, Mr. Toughguy?" It was the Kid.

Barrabas turned around.

"Now drop the gun, mister."

"And what if I don't, Kid?" He stared him in the eyes. Kid fired.

The bullet almost knocked him over as it chewed through his thigh. It didn't go deep into the leg, but it was painful. The impact made him drop his gun and grab the wound. But he stayed standing.

"That's what," said the Kid.

Major Braun stepped forward from behind a double-trunked pine. He had a smirk on his face and an Uzi in his hands.

"Finally, Barrabas, we are face-to-face, alone again." He seemed to forget about the Kid. "It amazes me how you got out of Cuba. It should have been impossible. You must tell me all about it...inside." He motioned to the Kid with the barrel of his submachine gun. "Let's go in. I'll radio to the other command quarters on the mainland for reinforcements. When they get here, we'll take care of Barrabas and his young friend."

CONSCIOUSNESS RETURNED SLOWLY to Tony Lopez. He lay somewhere with his eyes closed. He could hear the ocean, but he wasn't on the boat because there was no gentle rocking of the floor. It felt like bowling balls were rolling around inside his skull. The blood in his hair was sticky and cold. He could hardly move and didn't know why. Then he realized his hands and feet were tied, and his mouth was zipped up with tape. About all he could do was open his eyes, and even that required an immense effort.

He recognized the room immediately. He was back in the beach house where he'd been brought after X Command had lured him from Tampa airport. He was lying on the floor, but he could make out the map-covered walls and the radio set in one corner.

He strained against the ropes binding his feet and hands. They were tight, so tight that his hands were going a little numb. And the straining just made a whopper of a bowling ball crash back and forth against the walls of his skull. He flinched against the pain, and he realized he was crying. He gritted his teeth and strained again. The ropes didn't move.

Then he heard a voice in his head telling him to relax. He listened for it again. Relax. He relaxed. It was Emilio's voice. What would Emilio do, he asked himself. Relax, the answer came.

He allowed his body to go as limp as possible. He listened to the steady, even sound of the waves outside on the beach. He closed his eyes. The tension and the pain drained away.

He didn't know how long he stayed that way. He may have even fallen into unconsciousness again. He felt like he was floating on the steady, rolling waves that washed up on the beach. The waves were stroking him, calming him. They were warm. The voice told him to try his hands.

They moved. The ropes slipped around the wrists now as if they had grown looser. He knew that had happened because of the relaxation. He had lowered his blood pressure, forcing his body to shrink imperceptibly, but enough to make the bonds loosen.

He pulled his hands out of the loops until the rope was tight again. Once more he strained against them. Again they refused to budge. He listened to the waves. He did it three times, each time stretching the rope until he was able to twist his hand around and touch the knots with the fingers of his right hand.

He relaxed again and focused his concentration on his fingers, now numb from lack of blood. He could barely feel one of the knots. But barely was enough. The knot was tight, and he gripped it between his thumb and finger and wriggled it. It was a little less tight now. He tugged at it again.

It came loose.

After that it went quickly. In a few minutes his hands were free. The sudden rush of blood made them throb and ache. He had no time. He ripped the tape from his mouth and started on his feet.

The house was still completely silent when he finished. Careful not to make any noise, he stood up and went straight to the radio. He put the headphones over his ears and turned it on. He knew about CBs. He knew he could get out a call on this one. A call to the police.

The radio wasn't working. There was no static in the earphones. He looked at the panel. The phones weren't plugged in. He picked up the jack and aimed it for the socket.

The voice in his head said no. Suddenly he had an overpowering urge to get up and go outside. He tore the earphones off and walked to the door. Then he heard a shot.

The house was empty. He tiptoed down the hallway until he came to the living room. The wide windows looked out over the deck, the ocean and the pine forest.

Major Braun and the Kid were walking toward the stairs to the deck. Barrabas was in front of them, walking at gunpoint. He limped, his leg bleeding badly from the thigh.

Tony quickly looked around. He saw a handgun lying on the table by the couch. He recognized it from the movies. It was a Luger, with two swastikas engraved on the butt. He grabbed it. He hoped like hell it was loaded, since he didn't know how to check.

He ran through the door to the deck and looked down at the three men coming for the house. Holding the Luger in both hands he aimed for Major Braun's heart.

Tears poured from his eyes. He couldn't stop them. He was going to kill someone. His finger squeezed the hard, cold metal of the trigger. He fired, jerking his hand at the last moment. He cursed, in the face of evil, his failure of will.

The recoil stunned him, but not as much as the bullet stung Braun. It hit the hand that held the Uzi. The submachine gun flew into the air. Braun yelled and grabbed his hand.

Barrabas reacted.

He spun around on his good leg and with the back of his hand smashed the Kid across the face. It almost knocked him over. With the other hand he grabbed the Kid's M-16 to jerk it from his hand.

Braun looked up and saw Tony on the deck, still holding the Luger. Braun knew from the look in the boy's eyes that he wasn't going to shoot again. He ran for the stairs.

Tony heard him storming up the steps onto the deck. He pointed the gun at Braun as he came to the top of the stairs and backed away.

Braun took one look and decided not to bother. He ran into the beach house to radio for reinforcements.

Barrabas and the Kid were locked in combat on the ground below. Kid wouldn't let go of the rifle. He gripped it solidly with his hand and pushed against Barrabas. Barrabas fell back on his wounded leg, wincing as a hot current of pain jolted through his body. He heard himself groan as he fell. He pulled the rifle down with him, which in turn pulled the Kid on top. Bad move. Kid kneed him in the face.

Then Kid had a better idea. With both hands still gripping the contested M-16, he scrambled his legs around and aimed the toe of his boot for the wound in Barrabas's leg. Barrabas yelled in agony, and his nervous system went into shock mode. His grip on the gun weakened. Kid kicked again. Blood spurted over his boot. Suddenly, the sight of it made him savage. He kicked again and again. Barrabas let go of the gun and rolled away.

"Don't shoot! Don't shoot...or I'll kill you! I'll kill you!" Tony Lopez was shouting hysterically from the deck, pointing the Luger at the Kid. "Back off! I'll kill you, I swear. Get away from him!"

Kid had the M-16. He looked at Tony, then at Barrabas and back at Tony.

A loud explosion kaboomed from the house. Windows shattered and debris flew. Kid ran for the stairs.

At the top, Tony pointed the Luger at him, Kid ignored him, running into the house and down the hallway to the radio room.

The smoke had cleared.

The room looked like it'd been attacked by a killer tomato. Braun's legs and ass and a heap of guts sat in a chair that had been blown back against the wall. The rest of him was nowhere to be seen.

The Kid's friends were gone.

All he had now was his gun.

Outside, Barrabas gritted his teeth against the pain and with a Herculean effort of will pushed himself up from the ground. He grabbed Major Braun's discarded Uzi on the way.

He tested his weight on the wounded leg. It was like a live wire burning up through his groin. He had no choice. He took a deep breath, limped to the doorway and climbed.

Tony was at the top, white and frightened, clutching the Luger. He held it out.

"Kid went inside," Tony said. "He has the rifle still."

"Stella was right." Barrabas took the Luger. "You're different from your brother. You're not a killer. You don't know how lucky you are."

He limped slowly and painfully to the door of the house and leaned against the frame to take his weight off the leg.

"Kid!" he shouted inside. "You have a choice. You come out and throw down the gun ahead of you, you'll live."

There was no answer.

Then the Kid suddenly appeared in the living room. He was pale and breathing hard.

"Scum," he said flatly.

Barrabas didn't answer. He trained the Uzi on him. Kid's rifle hung at his side.

"Well, answer me, scum!" Kid shouted.

"What's your question, Kid?"

"Why scum like you get away with it?"

"With what?"

"Fouling up the world. Trying to stop people like me."

"From doing what?" Barrabas furrowed his brow to drive his concentration away from the agony rippling through his leg.

"I decide!" Kid was screaming now. "I decide who lives and who dies. I'm the judge. And I'm the executioner. Like I executed that Commie two days ago."

"What're you talking about?"

"That Commie! At his house in Tampa. You heard

about it. It's on the radio. His mother and brother got in the way so I killed them, too. It's war. A war against scum. And people gotta die."

He walked toward Barrabas.

"Drop the rifle, Kid." Barrabas raised his Uzi.

Kid stretched his arms out away from his sides with the M-16 in one hand. "There. See. I can't shoot now. Let me walk outside. Then we'll both throw our guns over the edge. Together. Otherwise I don't trust you."

Barrabas knew it was another goddamn trick. And he knew the only reason he went for it was to see what the trick was.

"Okay." He backed away from the door. "Very slowly," he warned.

Kid walked through the door.

They stood on the deck facing each other. Tony watched, frozen with fear. Barrabas held his Uzi in one arm like the Kid, and stuck it out over the edge of the deck. "Drop," he said.

"Fuck you," said the Kid.

He calmly turned and walked for the stairs.

"Kid," Barrabas called to him. Kid stopped and looked back. "Drop the rifle."

"I said, fuck you." He walked down the stairs and reappeared below the deck. He looked up at Barrabas. "It's mine!" He held the rifle up high. He started to walk away.

"Kid!" Barrabas yelled. The Kid stopped again. This time he didn't turn. "You have one last chance."

Kid paused a moment. He walked on.

Barrabas pulled the Luger from his belt. He noticed the swastikas on the handle.

"No!" Tony shouted.

Taking aim was one of the hardest things Barrabas had ever done.

The Kid, walking away from the beach house, was living in a fantasy world. He had massacred a Tampa family and run off to join the mercenaries so he could kill some more. Now he was walking away from it all. The Kid was nuts.

The bullet hit the kid in the back of the head. It was fast.

Barrabas dropped his arm and looked at Tony. The boy was crying. He wanted to go over and put his hand on Tony's shoulder and tell him it was all okay.

He couldn't.

Not now. Not the way he felt. He was just a killer. The Kid was dead.

He climbed painfully down the steps and walked to the road.

Soon, Tony followed.

Enter the
'Gear Up For Adventure Sweepstakes'
You May Win a 1986 AMC Jeep® CJ
Off-road adventure — Only in a Jeep.®

OFFICIAL RULES
No Purchase Necessary

1) To enter print your name, address and zip code on an Official Entry or on a 3" x 5" piece of paper. Enter as often as you choose but only one entry allowed to each envelope. Entries must be postmarked by January 17, 1986 and received by January 31, 1986. Mail entries first class. In Canada to Gold Eagle Gear Up For Adventure Sweepstakes, Suite 233, 238 Davenport Rd., Toronto, Ontario M5R 1J6. In the United States to Gold Eagle® Gear Up For Adventure Sweepstakes, P.O. Box 797, Cooper Station, New York, New York 10276. Sponsor is not responsible for lost, late, misdirected or illegible entries or mail. Sweepstakes open to residents 18 years or older at entry of Canada (except Quebec) and the United States. Employees and their immediate families and household of Harlequin Enterprises Limited, their affiliated companies, retailers, distributors, printers, agencies, American Motors Corporation and RONALD SMILEY INC. are excluded. This offer appears in Gold Eagle publications during the sweepstakes program and at participating retailers. All Federal, Provincial, State and local laws apply. Void in Quebec and where prohibited or restricted by law.

2) First Prize awarded is a 1986 Jeep CJ with black soft top and standard equipment. Color and delivery date subject to availability. Vehicle license, driver license, insurance, title fees and taxes are the winner's responsibility. The approximate retail value is $8,500 U.S./$10,625 Canadian. 10 Second Prizes awarded of a Sports Binocular. The approximate retail value is $90 U.S./$112.50 Canadian. 100 Third Prizes awarded of Gold Eagle Sunglasses. The approximate retail value is $6.95 U.S./$8.65 Canadian. No substitution, duplication or cash redemption of prizes. First Prize distributed from U.S.A.

3) Winners will be selected in random drawings from all valid entries under the supervision of RONALD SMILEY INC. an independent judging organization whose decisions are final. Odds of winning depend on total number of entries received. First prize winner will be notified by certified mail and must return an Affidavit of Compliance within 10 days of notification. Winner residents of Canada must correctly answer a time-related arithmetical skill-testing question. Affidavits and prizes that are refused or undeliverable will result in alternate winners randomly drawn. The First Prize winner may be asked for the use of their name and photo without additional compensation. Income tax and other taxes are prize winners' responsibility.

4) For a major prize winner list, Canadian residents send a stamped, self addressed envelope to Gold Eagle Winner Headquarters, Suite 157, 238 Davenport Road, Toronto, Ontario M5R 1J6. United States residents send a stamped, self-addressed envelope to Gold Eagle Winner Headquarters, P.O. Box 182, Bowling Green Station, New York, NY 10274. Winner list requests may not include entries and must be received by January 31, 1986 for response.

A division of
WORLDWIDE LIBRARY®

GOLD EAGLE